THREE-CORNERED WAR

THREE-CORNERED WAR

RICHARD WORMSER

WILDSIDE PRESS

Published by Wildside Press LLC.
www.wildsidebooks.com

I

Water bubbled from the base of the big rock, and ran through a natural channel in the sandstone, down to the river. Twenty years before a passing homesteader had admired this, and seen in it a chance to provide his home with a luxury few Westerners had—running water.

So he had built below the big rock, and Rock Spring had been born.

Now it had three hundred people and a well-cherished rumor that the railroad was on its way.

One big general store, one big saloon—and one little blind tiger for the Indians—one hotel, one law officer.

One gambler, too; one of the tables in Wellman's Great Chance, the saloon, was baize covered for his use.

Dan Younge was the gambler just now, and a very good one, a very nice guy: good-looking, strong, even-tempered. You might have taken him for a young rancher or a horse-breaker, or a mining engineer, if it weren't for his clothes and the fact that he had no friends.

No friend, and, of course, no girl, in the usual sense of the word. Nobody ever saw a married gambler, and women were too scarce in the West for a respectable girl to waste her time falling in love with a man who wasn't going to marry her.

There was one law officer, and that was Jack Romayne, the sheriff. He'd gotten the job by being pleasant, both to the rich and the poor, and also by winning a turkey shoot one time.

It had never occurred to anyone in Rock Spring to ask Jack how many gunfights he'd been in. If they had, he probably would have told the truth, which was that he'd never even seen a gun battle.

That was Rock Spring. Dan Younge didn't mind being its

gambler, and Jack Romayne believed himself lucky to be its sheriff.

Until the wagon came walking into Union Street behind two pretty good horses, with the reins tied up to the whipsocket.

Six men lay dead in that wagon, and they had not died of old age. They had been carbine shot. And they had been scalped.

Smelling feed and water and the company of their kind, the two horses turned into the Square Deal Livery stable and stopped at the watering trough, fighting their check lines to get down to the water.

So it was the hostler at the stable who saw the bodies first, and the whoop he let out sounded from one end of Union Street to the other. Jack Romayne, making out delinquent tax notices in the sheriff's office, heard it, and at first he thought it was a kid-noise, boys playing one of their mock-murder games.

But when it was repeated, it was over the sounds of running feet, and Jack jumped up and ran, too. He buckled on his gun-belt as he went, and later he could not say why; few daytime errands in Rock Springs called for an armed sheriff.

He took one look in the wagon bed and said: "Get the Indian agent, somebody. You, Dan. Go get Major Miles."

Dan Younge nodded and turned away, a cool man, one who had seen a lot and didn't bother to talk much.

But the rest of the townsmen weren't like that. As soon as Jack had spoken up, they all started a chorus: "Injuns. Yessir, redskins. Them Shoshones did this!"

Jack Romayne nodded at the wagon-wide entrance to the livery yard. "Some of you go stand guard there," he said. "Keep any women and kids out. This isn't for them."

But the men just stood there, and he had to call them by name. "Hostetter, Wellman, Sydnor. Take charge of that gate there!"

They were all older men than he, store owners and mortgage holders.

Sydnor stared before he went to help Hostetter and Wellman

keep the arch closed.

Dan Younge came back then. "Here's Major Miles, Jack," he said. "And I thought maybe you could use the Doc, too." He had Dr. Arnall in tow.

"Thanks," Jack Romayne said. "I guess I should have thought of that."

Dan shrugged. "Certainly not much a doctor can do for them now." He leaned against the tie rail by the water trough and watched.

Charley Sydnor came back from the entrance, unable to miss anything. "Going to get up a posse, Sheriff?"

Jack Romayne looked at him, a stocky man, and one of the biggest taxpayers in town. "Why," Jack drawled, "I thought I'd ask for volunteers—to ride out in the country one at a time and maybe see what was happening."

Major Miles had never been in the Army; the title went with the Indian agent job. He peered into the wagon and said: "I don't believe it. I just don't believe it."

Jack Romayne said: "Indian job, doc?"

The doctor shrugged. "I don't know as I ever saw a scalping before," he said. "Maybe you ought to ask the major. He's more knowing on Indian than me."

Miles twisted up his red face and squinted at the doctor. Finally he decided not to take offense. He said: "Never saw a scalping before, either. And I don't know as how my Shoshones have. Any man wanted to kill someone and throw it off on Indians could use a knife."

"Who else?" Sydnor asked. "If it wasn't Indians, who else?"

Jack Romayne said, "I'd like to look the wagon over first. Afterwards'll be time enough to put a name on things." He grabbed the near horse's bridle. "I'm taking them over to the undertaker's, to Doc Beals'. Anybody wants to come along can help me unload."

They faded away, then, and Jack led the team across the street, and up the alley and to the back of Doc Beals', where the hearse was, and the little shed with Doc's horses and the big cans of stuff that Doc used.

The sheriff's office backed on the same alley, and Jack told Doc to bring the wagon down there when he was finished. He went to the sheriff's shed and pulled down some hay for his two horses, the pack horse and the trail horse, and he went into his own office through the unlocked back door and rolled himself a cigarette.

The notices of unpaid taxes were still on his desk, but they didn't matter now. Trouble had come to Rock Spring—bad trouble.

It didn't matter who had killed those men. Maybe they hadn't even been killed in his county, but it would be up to him to get the killers. There wasn't anybody else.

He smiled, but not with pleasure. About two years ago the U. S. Marshal had been through here, had looked over the town, and had ended up deputizing Jack Romayne. The badge was in the safe someplace.

He opened the safe and finally found it. It was in a box with his Deputy United States Marshal commission, and a schedule of fees he was to get if there was ever any Federal work to be done.

There was just himself. Fat fools like Charley Sydnor could bawl around about wanting to serve on a posse, but Jack Romayne would lead that posse. It was what he was paid for.

Doc Beals came to the door. "Here's your wagon, Sheriff. I told my boys not to wash it out. That was right, wasn't it?"

Jack Romayne said: "That was just fine, Doc."

He couldn't even run away, he was thinking. The very thing he wanted to run away from had closed all the roads.

II

Dan Younge was thinking the same thing; that the roads out of town were closed. He had been planning on leaving that day, as soon as he could get Wellman aside and draw his money.

But the trails were now closed.

He went into the Great Chance and drifted past the bar and the gambling tables to the kitchen, helped himself to a cup of coffee, threw a casual thanks at the Chinese cook and went to sit on the back porch near the potato bin.

Then he went out on the street. Charley Sydnor had left the livery yard and was in his store; he could see the merchant sticking out his gold watch chain at a couple of young wives, while a clerk unrolled bolt goods.

So Dan Younge went up the street, up to the last house before the big rock. Then he turned right, as though going for a stroll into the country; circled and so came to the back door of the Sydnor house.

It was not locked. Rock Spring was an honest and peaceful town. He went through the kitchen and into the hall; he knew his way.

She was in the living room, darning Charley Sydnor's socks. But she dropped the darning at once and stood up and came toward him, raising her mouth for his kiss, pressing all her body against him.

She was fourteen years younger than Charley, a tall woman with a proud way of carrying herself that should have warned the storekeeper.

Dan Younge skillfully ran his fingers over Phyllis Sydnor's strong and resilient back. In a strange town, in search of the only diversion that meant anything to him, Dan Younge always looked up the richest man in town; if he had a pretty wife it was a cinch.

"Let's go upstairs," he said. "It's two hours till Charley's mealtime."

"You could set your watch by him," Phyllis said.

He turned and shoved her a little ahead of him, and she went, slowly at first and then almost running the last few feet to the stairs.

III

As always, there were three or four men sitting around the sheriff's office. They had elected him, and they chose to think of his office as a sort of exclusive club. Hostetter, of the feed store, was there; Wellman, who owned the Great Chance; Shurtz, the hotel man; all merchants big enough to have clerks to run their prosperous business for them.

Now they looked at Jack Romayne, these sachems of counter and cash drawer, and Hostetter said: "Well, sheriff?"

Jack Romayne shook his head. "Nothing in the wagon to say was it white or Indians did the trick. The brands on the horses are some I never saw before. You know as much as I do."

"I sure hate to start an Indian scare," Wellman said. "Next thing you know, the trails'll stay closed for a year or more. We'll be cut off from fresh supplies, from trade, from everything."

Hostetter said: "Suppose what was done to those men was done by whites; you think that's gonna fill travelers with ease and confidence?"

Jack Romayne said: "If it's Indians, maybe we ought to wait for the Army." He added: "If the dead men were on the reservation, what were they doing there? Trespassing? Molesting Indian women? Bootlegging, maybe?"

Hostetter's voice was filled with contempt. "It seems we picked up an Indian lover for a sheriff. Well, we put you in office—we can take you out."

Jack Romayne glared it him, but then Doc Beals came tumbling in the back door, holding his clenched hand in front of him. "Look," he said. "Look what I found inside one of those fellas' boots. Just look." He opened his hand, and it glittered. It was full of gold nuggets.

Hostetter said, slowly: "Those Indians are no fools. If there's gold on their land, they'll lose that land. It's happened every time."

There was noise out on the street. Major Miles was tying his horse to the sheriff's rail, while Sydnor watched him. The Major, fussy in small things, took his time about it, and then the two men marched into the office.

"I heard about the gold," Major Miles said. "If those men were on the reservation, mining, they were outside the law."

Sydnor said: "And if they were someplace else, whoever jumped their claim has sure seen to it that there won't be many prospectors out for awhile."

"Send for the Army," Jack Romayne said. "It's the only thing to do."

Wellman said, quickly: "We don't want that. Don't want some Army finance officer fixing prices, commandeering supplies."

They all turned to Sydnor. The stout man said: "Wagons leave tracks. Tracks for sheriffs to follow."

"Thanks," Jack Romayne said, and went out to saddle his horses. Then he went back into the office and got a rifle, .30-.30, from the rack. He locked the rack again, and tossed the key in his hand. "I'd better leave this here," he said. "I'd better deputize someone, too."

Five pairs of cold eyes stared back at him. He said, suddenly: "Sydnor, raise your right hand."

Sydnor said: "Young man…"

"I'm not a young man," Jack Romayne said. "I'm a badge with a body behind it. There's a difference. Your right hand, Sydnor."

IV

Dan Younge pulled a cheroot out of his pocket, put it between his lips and then said: "Sorry. Almost forgot," and put it back in his pocket.

From the dressing table Phyllis Sydnor said: "Go on and smoke."

"What'll you tell Sydnor? That you've taken up cheroots for the asthma he knows you don't have?"

"I'll tell him to go to hell."

Dan Younge's gambler face froze. He'd known this was coming, but when he had learned this morning that the trails were closed, he had hoped against hope. He said: "He treats you all right, looking at it from a money point of view. Lot of ladies'd give a quarter inch off their eyelashes to have the run of Sydnor's store."

She ran her hands down the Belgian lace on her shirtwaist. "Money!" she said. "Do you think I'd sell myself for money?"

Yep, Dan Younge answered her. But he kept it to himself. Time had come for the roofless wanderer act. He said: "When you're in the dark, in a strange town, any lamp looks pretty. Once you own the house, you begin wondering whether you shouldn't have ordered a different kind of lampshade from Sears Roebuck."

Sharpness was coming in under her voice. "What does all that mean?"

Good. If he got her mad, an exit was still possible. "Maybe it means I envy you, having a home, not having to worry, even if Charley Sydnor's in that home with you. Me, what have I got? A spare suit, a seat at a poker table, a hotel room."

It was good, but she hadn't been listening. "I'd like you to stay. Stay, while I tell him…"

Dan Younge got off the windowsill, stood looking down at her. "You don't know what happened downtown today, then. Do you?"

She shook her head, her eyes wide, staring at him. There was enough suspicion in her eyes to make Dan Younge begin to believe that this was not the first time she had heard a man tell the tale; but he had never exacted previous innocence from his ladies.

He said: "We can't get out of town, lady. Not today, and I don't know when." Quickly, he told her what had happened, about the wagon, about the men.

She hardly seemed to be listening to him. When he finished, she said: "Good! Oh, good! We'll stay here and tell Charley Sydnor to do his worst. I'll move down to the hotel with you."

"Sydnor owns this town," Dan Younge pointed out. "I don't want you hurt, lady."

Suddenly her anger, her fire went out of her. "I go soft all over when you call me that," she said. "Nobody ever called me lady before."

He had a part to play. Maybe he could still find a way to leave her with her dignity, to leave her thinking that he departed with regret and a picture of her in his heart. He said: "You think I don't have feelings? We've got to figure out what's best for you. I'll scout downtown, find out if the Army's coming, what's going to happen. This whole thing may blow over."

She said: "You're so wise, so smart," and for just a moment he thought she was laughing at him. But she wasn't, and he headed for the back stairs and out.

He did not go to the bar or the sheriff's office, where news might be found; instead he headed at once for the livery stable, gave orders for his horse to have oats, for more grain to be packed in his trail bags, for his bill to be gotten ready. The whis-key-reeking hostler tried to tell him nobody was leaving town, but he walked away.

At the hotel he packed, rolling his extra suit carefully in

canvas against dust. He paid his bill there and went to the stable and got on his horse.

He headed now for the sheriff's office, but then he saw Jack Romayne, the sheriff, riding toward Sydnor's store—alone, leading a packhorse.

He swore. You'd have thought that even in a little town like Rock Spring there would be one man with enough gumption to offer to go with the sheriff.

Besides the town gambler.

V

Jack Romayne had led his white packhorse around to Sydnor's store and tied the two animals to Sydnor's rail. The saddle horse promptly started chewing on the wood. Romayne slapped his nose and went on into the store.

He grabbed two gunny sacks from a pile Sydnor had for sale, and started throwing canned goods and sacks of dry stuff into the burlap.

Ellen Lea, who clerked for Sydnor, came over. "Let me help you, Jack."

He looked at her. She was a widow, thought not yet twenty-five; Brad Lea had tried to get rich in the windmill business, and his ambition had driven him up a tower in a bad wind. The gold wedding ring she still wore was darker than her hair, and her eyes were a light, prairie-searching blue. Perhaps because of her coloration, she seemed to keep herself neater than most of the women in Rock Spring; even in the spring winds she never had the slightly dusty look of most prairie people.

He said: "I can handle it, Ellen."

Ellen Lea said: "You're going out on the prairie?"

"Your boss and mine, the Honorable Charles Sydnor, just reminded me of how much salary this county has paid me. I'm going to go earn it."

She said: "Let me get a boy to help you load."

"I'll do it."

But she followed him out to the horses, watched while he put a sack on each side of the packhorse, and then helped him by going to the off side and stowing things in the saddlebag. When both saddlebags were full he tied the necks of the half empty gunny sacks together, and lashed them tight.

"That ought to hold."

He moved to mount, but she put a hand on his arm. "Jack, tell them."

"Tell them what? That they're asking me to die for my measly salary? They couldn't care. Their businesses are threatened."

She shook her head. "I don't know what it was I wanted you to tell them."

Jack Romayne said: "Listen, Ellen. Brad's been gone six months. When I get back, eat supper with me at the hotel once in awhile."

He turned without waiting for an answer, and swung into the saddle. When he was down against the leather, he looked at her.

Her head was up, and the light blue eyes had more shine than he had seen in a while. She said, "I'll be proud to, Jack."

He nodded and picked up his lines. The packhorse set back a little as usual, and Jack rode over and slapped at his rump with his saddle lines.

He said: "So long, Ellen," and then realized that another rider had come up.

Dan Younge, the gambler, said: "I hope there's grub enough for two."

Jack Romayne looked him over. Younge wore the neat black clothes of his trade, but he had switched from varnished black gaiters to heavy cowhide boots. There was a rifle under his left leg, and a bedroll behind the saddle. "Rock Spring bores me, sheriff. Let's go get some fresh air."

Ellen Lea laughed suddenly, and the two men rode out, Dan Younge turning to sweep his black hat at her. They rode down the street, made a turn, following the canyon flood, and were out of the little town.

Jack Romayne was already bent in the saddle, watching the tracks of the wagon that had come into town.

VI

Second Lieutenant James V. Beer and Sergeant Rylan rode at the head of the column of twos. Two troopers were out ahead as advance, one on each side of the column. From time to time the sergeant would glance at the sun and blow his whistle, and the pickets would drop back, fall into column behind the leaders, and be relieved by whichever pair had been eating dust at the tail of the blue snake.

Suddenly, Trooper Strayne, on right picket, stood in his stirrups, raised his hand, and circled. At once, Mr. Beer threw up his own hand and pulled it down hard, clenching his fist. The column accepted the signal to halt quietly, and Beer rode off to the right front.

"Sit tight in your saddle," Sergeant Rylan said. "Keep your feet in your stirrups. Anybody in doubt, check his carbine for ready."

Two or three of the men took their short rifles from the scabbards and snicked the breech mechanisms.

When Mr. Beer reached Strayne, the trooper silently pointed to the ground. The lieutenant got down and examined the hoof prints his soldier had discovered. Then he grunted, said, "Nice work, Strayne. They were almost dusted in. Two men, riding shod horses, probably yesterday."

He squatted by the prints, musing, looked up after a moment and said: "Go send the sergeant up here. And tell him the men can stand easy."

Strayne saluted, and took off in a skittering run down the sand dune. His officer, left alone, heard the deep mutter of Sergeant Rylan's voice: "Stand down. Every man loosen his horse's girth, and go light on your canteens." Then there was the sound of the sergeant's mount trotting up the sandhill.

Beer took out a sack of tobacco and a pad of papers and built himself a careful cigarette. He wet it down thoroughly with spit before lighting it, relieving a little the burning acridity of long dried tobacco.

When Rylan dismounted, Beer handed him the makings and pointed at the track.

Sergeant Rylan said: "Hundred to one they are not Indians, sir."

"My thinking, Rylan. But we're deep in the reservation. This is supposed to be closed to miners and settlers."

Rylan contented himself with a "Yes, sir." He lit his cigarette, passed the tobacco and paper back.

Mr. Beer unbuttoned a shirt pocket under his unbuttoned blouse and stowed his smoking away. Shaving on patrol was not an everyday thing; as he ran a hand up his cheek, the scrape of his whiskers was loud in his ear. He said, finally: "Our job, I guess. If we find out—as we shall—that they were just cowboys taking a short cut, we'll be in dry country with nothing to show for it."

"Yes, sir."

Beer sighed. "Someday I'd like to try this patrolling with light equipment—a canteen, some pemmican, ammunition—to each man, and light horses that could live off the prairie."

Sergeant Rylan said: "That's not the Army way." Both men rose, stepped back into their saddles and walked down to the waiting troop.

The sergeant got the men back into their saddles, the lieutenant gave his orders. "Fast trot. The sooner we overtake our men, the less ground we'll have to backtrack on."

Rylan said: "Fast trot, hoooh!" and the patrol moved out.

Half an hour later they hit lava rock and the tracks petered out. Lieutenant Beer led them back to their original line of march.

VII

Jack Romayne let the packhorse loose when they were a mile from town, winding the end of the lead rope around the hitch of the packsaddle. Once the beast made up his mind he was going to have to go, he went; a few feet behind Jack's horse, at a steady amble that ate up miles.

Jack said: "A hell of a thing, when all a man gets to help him is a gambler."

Plains dust was already soiling the gambler's black hat. He said: "Oh, don't thank me for coming along. There's nothing very pure or great about it."

The sheriff stared at the choice of words. "Pure?" he said. "Great? You trying to make fun of me, Younge?"

Dan Younge said: "Fun is not a thing you can expect to come out of Rock Spring anytime in the year. The water and the soil're not right for growing it."

Romayne shrugged. "All Rock Spring grows is money for Sydnor."

Younge grunted. "I'd like to get him in a poker game. But he's too cute."

Out here, this far from town, kids did not bring the milk cows and the saddle horses of Rock Spring to graze. The short thick prairie grass took a track and held it; the marks of the wagon wheels were plain to read. "Heading for reservation country," Jack Romayne said and straightened in the saddle, no longer forced to bend down to read the trail. He gestured ahead, and the twin lines could be seen in the grass for a half mile ahead. "Let's make a little time."

They put their horses to the job and moved along silently for a long spell; the sun moved well to their left, and their shadows got long on the land. Then Jack Romayne said: "There," and pulled up. "It couldn't have been much farther," he said.

Dan Younge said: "I don't see."

Romayne pointed. "There was a saddle horse tied behind the wagon up to here," he said. "This isn't a road; it's just open prairie. Somebody drove the wagon to here, then got out and rode back. See?" He pointed to the tracks. "They would have to bring the wagon this far, or the horses would turn back to the nearest water hole. But the wind's from the south almost always now, and the teams would smell Rock Spring and head for it. He knew horses, whoever he was."

Dan Younge said: "But why? He was going to a lot of trouble to see those miners got to a town that could give them burial."

"Decent burial," Jack Romayne said. "The other kind anybody with a shovel could give them." He squinted at the sky. "Not much day left," he said. "Couple of hours. Our friend had no shoes on his horse. Which could mean Indian."

"Who else?" The gambler stood in his stirrups. "I'm soft. Been in one town too long. Who else? No white man around don't at least put shoes on the back feet."

"Could be someone who pulled the shoes to make it look like Indians."

Dan Younge shook his head. "Never knew it to fail," he said. "Pin a star on a man, and right away he gets himself a suspicious nature."

They rode, and after a while they had almost ridden the sun out of the sky. They squinted at the sandhills for bearings so they could pick up their trail in the morning. Then they gave the horses their heads, and soon came to a little spring to make their camp by.

Sage brush roots make a good fire, and there was plenty to eat on the packhorse. Dan Younge sighed and rolled himself a cigarette. "From the grub you brought along, you must be planning a long campout."

"No. I was just hitting at Charley Sydnor the only way you can hurt him; money. He'd sooner I took his wife than groceries out of his stock." Romayne lit his own cigarette and added: "Pretty woman, too. Wonder how come she married old Sydnor?"

"Woman has to marry someone," Dan Younge said mildly. "If she likes to eat. Sydnor's got groceries."

"Yeah, I guess so… Isn't that something moving out in the brush?"

"Coyote, prob'ly… You and that Ellen Lea see much of each other?"

Jack Romayne said: "Well, no. Her husband was killed six months ago. You were in Rock Spring then, weren't you?… I aim to see a lot more of her when I get back." He paused, and at once added: "If I get back… This is no trip to the corner saloon. Those men in the wagon…" He broke off.

Dan Younge said: "I saw them."

"All right. So we had a nice ride today, sunshine, fresh air, good company. But we're out here in the middle of a reservation, no roads, nobody but us two—and either a tribe of Indians on the warpath—or somebody good enough to kill and scalp six strong men."

Dan Younge said: "You make it sound pleasant. A nice ride in the sun."

Jack Romayne chunked a couple of sage roots into the fire. Their fuzzy outer layer flared up, and then the roots themselves caught and settled down to burning, slowly. He said: "You didn't have to come. Why did you?"

"It was time to leave Rock Spring," the gambler said. "It seemed safer to leave with you."

The sheriff's laugh was a hard thing against the prairie night. "If safe was what you wanted, you should have put up with Rock Spring a while. You must have gotten a real hate for that town."

"No. It was just time to move on."

"That's the itchiest foot I ever…"

The bullet came out of the night, and that was all you could say of it. It hit the sage-root fire—it takes a good gun not to aim at a fire in the night—and scattered brands around the little camp. Dan Younge was busy knocking one off his shoulder before it burnt through his shirt; he didn't see Jack Romayne make a sliding lunge and shove sand onto what was left of the blaze, using his boots as scrapers.

They had picketed the packhorse, turned the other two out to graze. Now they could hear the animal fighting his picket line, rearing and whickering, and then the gun on the prairie spoke again, or maybe it was two guns this time.

One of the bullets thudded into the sand near the piled saddles; the other one found a target somewhere along Jack Romayne's side, and it carried enough force to roll him over, into the char-studded area of the fire.

Then there was the thudding noise of horses going away, fast.

Dan Younge got his feet under him, checked his belt gun to make sure it hadn't fallen out when he hit the dirt and started running to where they'd picketed one of the horses.

He wasn't thinking of the odds against running the men down, it was good not to think about odds once in awhile.

But he wasn't twenty yards from the camp when a wail, back by the fire, stopped him.

It hardly had words at first. Then, stopped, he could hear better; the sounds began to resolve themselves into: "Help," and "Don't leave me," and "I'm hurt bad."

So he turned and went back. There was a little glow left to the shot-up fire; it showed him Jack Romayne, thrashing around on the sand. He knelt and struck a match. "All right, Jack. I didn't know they got you."

The sheriff moaned softly.

The match showed blood, not much but some, high on Jack Romayne's shirt. Dan Younge used his knife to cut the cloth away, lit another match. He said: "Bullet went in, but not far, came out again under your arm there. It couldn't have hit bone."

But by then the air had gotten to the hole. Jack Romayne let out a scream that was a masterpiece.

Dan Younge said nothing. They had had a pile of chunks ready for the fire; he piled them together, lit them, and used the already torn shirt to make a tight bandage, always working silently. When he was done, he put the coffee pot—somehow it had not turned over—on the flames and said: "A cup of hot coffee, and you'll live."

Jack Romayne took the tin cup of coffee when it was handed to him, and swore at the heat. "We'll have to head back for Rock Spring tomorrow. I hope we don't run into trouble on the way; it'd all be up to you."

"And a gambler's not much of a reed to lean on in a wrangle."

"I didn't say that. You better see if the packhorse is still there."

Dan Younge stared across the fire at the sheriff. Then he shrugged and got up and walked out past the circle of light and on, blinking a little, to where they had picketed the horse. It was there.

He came back, nodded, and started spreading his blankets for the night.

"Hope they didn't run off the others," Jack Romayne said.

"Sure, sheriff, sure."

"How many horses did it sound like to you, when they was going away?"

"I couldn't count," Dan Younge said. "We'll know in the morning."

"Maybe they couldn't find both our horses. Or either of them… If we can find one, we can saddle the packhorse, he's rough but pretty strong."

And if we can't, Dan Younge thought, bet you count on your star and your wound to ride while I walk.

He stretched out between the blankets, rolled on his back, looked at the stars. Jack Romayne was saying something in his grumbling voice, but Dan Younge pretended to be asleep.

Then the streak in him that had kept him a gambler all his life came up and took over, and he found himself grinning at the sky. You paid to draw, Dan, he told himself, and you didn't fill. This jackleg sheriff was a fine one to draw to; you'd have done a lot better to stay in Rock Spring and take your chances with the grocer and his lady.

Then, before he slept, he thought, Those were white men that bushwhacked us. Indians—no Indians I've ever heard of fight at night.

VIII

The command was up an hour before dawn, with no order from Lieutenant Beer who lay, happy in his bedroll, while Sergeant Rylan got wood and water details out and working. When Lieutenant Beer finally pulled out and shoved his feet into his high boots, water was bubbling on his personal fire, there was bacon and coffee and pilot biscuit laid out for him to eat, his horse had been brought in and was being grained and curried—life on a prairie patrol was almost pleasant for him. He decided to shave. His striker held a bull's eye for him, and they broke camp and marched out just as the first edge of the sun hit the rolling horizon.

This was the second edge of the triangular ride he'd laid out for himself. Tonight they'd camp at Summer Waters—coordinate 64.42-31.28 on the maps Beer had made for the regiment—and then tomorrow be riding straight for home.

If nothing happened, Lieutenant Beer said it in his mind, like knocking wood, and then said it again, in a sentence: If nothing happens, I'll be in quarters tomorrow night, with a reading lamp and my books, and the plan for a three squadron cavalry regiment that I'm working on.

The first heat of the day was beginning to roll across the land. He unbuttoned the top button of his shirt, under his neckerchief, and settled down in the saddle, slumping a little, letting his weight come down on the broad stirrups and the shock of the trot break in his shoulders.

It was not a bad life. Every month he stayed out here, every patrol he made, would go into his personal file, part of his permanent record... The Army followed the English system, where an officer joined a regiment and stayed with it until he made general officer, if ever, instead of the files system coming into use on the Continent, but there were exceptions.

General Staff, Department Staff, War College all drew men from the field, the regiments. A good adjutant, with plenty of troop command and field work behind him was certain to get a chance at one of the three, and later on a field record was necessary in your docket if you didn't want to get labeled a red-tape expert.

I'm twenty-three, Jim Beer thought. If I have to stay with troops till I'm thirty, all right. There's plenty of time on these wilderness posts to study, and no temptation to spend your pay on anything much but books and…

Sergeant Rylan said: "Lieutenant," and ended his reverie.

The sergeant was standing in his stirrups and pointing the way Lieutenant Beer had taught his men to point—arm straight out, fingers spread. The lieutenant pulled his command to a halt and sighted along Rylan's arm and through the notch of his fingers, and so saw what the sergeant had seen at once without unnecessary talk.

There was a column of dust rising off the prairies, and while he watched, it progressed across the space between Rylan's middle finger and his ring finger.

Beer squinted hard, and then brought up his field glasses. The thing at the base of the column of dust was white, and—unless they had found that rare thing, an albino buffalo—that meant a horse.

Lieutenant Beer said: "Corporal Horne, take the two first troopers and scout. If you get into a fight, squeeze your shots off raggedly and we'll come to your help. If it's safe, give it three rapid rounds, and we'll join you."

At once Horne and the first pair of soldiers pulled out of column and put their horses at the run. The lieutenant nodded to himself; he'd issued that order with the promptness he required of himself.

He passed the order to Sergeant Rylan to move out, and the file took up patrol again. He made no effort to order eyes front;

every man rode with his gaze on Horne and the two troopers… Rechter and Sully, their names were.

The dust raised by the three soldiers moved fast towards the dust raised by the unknown and then the latter died down and was gone. Whoever was with the white horse had stopped, and was waiting to be met; but whether his intention—or their intention—was friendly or not remained to be seen.

Beer said quietly: "Sergeant, the men had better check their carbines. If Horne needs us, he'll need us fast."

"Yes, sir." But instead of shouting the order, Sergeant Rylan passed it back along the line quietly; he was listening for the sound of gunfire.

It came as the clicking of the carbines ended: three fast shots. There was too much dust to see the powder smoke.

Lieutenant Beer said: "Column, left oblique, march. At the gallop, march."

Rylan relayed the orders in a booming shout, and they took off, riding hard, horses and men alike glad to be moving out of the dull trot.

Lieutenant Beer pulled up with a dash at the group. His corporal, Horne, was down off his horse and so were Rechter and Sully, and for the moment their blue bodies kept him from seeing anything more than the white horse, nosing at the two troop mounts, trying to decide whether to make friends. The civilian animal was haltered instead of bridled, and his lead rope had been twisted to make a sort of hackamore.

Then a man pushed through between Horne and Sully and came towards him—a thin man, about thirty, in black clothes that were now pretty dust-stained. He limped as he walked. "Lieutenant, I'm Dan Younge." While Beer was still deciding whether to put out his hand or not, the man Younge put his own up, and they shook.

The lieutenant said his own name and rank, and waited.

Dan Younge said: "You're a grateful sight, Lieutenant Beer. You and your men." He laughed. "I'm not much for walking at its twilight best, and in this sun and with these boots…" He grinned. "I'll give it to you straight—your corporal said to save it for you. We were bushwhacked last night, the sheriff there and I. He got himself wounded. Not bad."

Lieutenant Beer got down from his horse. He gestured at his canteen, but Dan Younge shook his head, flicked a thumb at the white horse's pommel.

The lieutenant said: "You're aware you're on Indian land." It was not a question.

Dan Younge said: "Sure. Indian Agent Miles at Rock Spring was one of the fellas sent Sheriff Romayne out here."

"I'd better talk to the sheriff himself. You may be under arrest. Civilian peace officers on Indian reservations are way off bounds."

Dan Younge stopped smiling. Then he said: "Take it easy, mister. Me and one wounded sheriff aren't enough to really rile the U.S. Army, are they? Well, anyway, things were quiet and peaceful in Rock Spring, you might say, with the rich getting richer and the poor working for them, when this wagon came rolling into town…"

He went on with the story. Lieutenant Beer listened to it quietly, but he was summing this Dan Younge up. The clothes were not those of a cowboy; in fact, only pastors and gamblers favored black in this dust covered country. It was a fair-to-middling certainty that Dan Younge was not the Reverend anything… He was finishing his story.

Lieutenant Beer said: "I'll talk to Romayne." There was a good, broad chance here that Younge was somehow involved in the shooting. Nothing about professional gamblers that Jim Beer knew inspired much respect for them; but, then, what did he know? Before he had been a cavalryman he had been a cadet, and before that a kid in a Hudson valley town. He didn't know that there had ever been a gambler in Vlietville, though the men sometimes played poker in the back of the barbershop.

He reserved judgment. "Sheriff, I'm Lieutenant James

Beer." He named his regiment.

Romayne said: "Well, didn't you get the story from Dan Younge there? I'm a sick man, lieutenant, and that packhorse of mine's a rough goer. Rough as they come and…"

Lieutenant Beer had made his decision: "All right. We'll take you back to where you camped last night, rescue what we can of your gear, and escort you back to Rock Spring. You can ride one of our horses. The troopers'll have to take turns trailing from another man's stirrup."

He couldn't quite hear the groan that went up from the file. Almost, but not quite. Rylan was barking at Trooper Harris to give up his horse and be the first trailer.

The lieutenant said: "If there are gold miners trespassing on the reservation, I'll have to do something about it. Corporal Horne, ride for the fort. I'll give you a note in writing."

Dan Younge said: "I'll go with him."

"I think not," Lieutenant Beer said. "That white packhorse couldn't keep up with a cavalry mount, and I've no intention of detaching one of my horses permanently. Anyway, Younge, I'm curious to know why you were so anxious to get away from Rock Spring."

"It's a reason they never taught you at West Point," Dan Younge said, and grinned again.

The lieutenant wrote his note and gave it to the corporal and Rylan moved the detachment out. Dan Younge rode the white horse now, and seemed content enough.

IX

Rock Spring had quieted down some after Romayne and Dan Younge rode out. Sydnor sat around the sheriff's office a few minutes, tossing the deputy's badge in the palm of his hand, then tossed the badge to Wellman. "You're deputy," he said. "You like that sort of thing." He walked to the door of the office, his firm steps and heavy weight shaking the wind-dried build-ing. "Consider yourself sworn in." He left.

Wellman looked after him. "Charley's mighty sudden act-ing," he said. "I don't think it's legal for a representative to hold county office."

Hostetter shrugged. "Won't do any great harm," he said. "Not much sheriffing to do. Wasn't that your gambler that rode out with Romayne?"

Wellman said: "I wasn't looking. Dan Younge, you mean? It don't seem likely."

"That gambler's pretty smart," Shurtz said. He fumbled in his pocket till he found one of his constant hoard of licorice drops, popped it into his mouth, rolled it around. "Maybe Jack Romayne's not so dumb, either. They've gone off looking for the gold, of course."

It was a new thought. Wellman and Hostetter stared at him.

Shurtz nodded. "Sure. Romayne didn't want to go, then he went, awful quiet, for him. Gold, that's what come into his mind. Came into mine, too. I may take a crack at it, yet."

Hostetter said: "Shurtz has a plan."

"Well, I been thinking," Shurtz said. His voice had risen a little. "Supposing I was to say I'd figured out where this gold strike is?"

At once he had their interest.

He said: "Now. It ain't on the part of the reservation that

touches town; if it was, the wagon couldn't a come in the way it did. It came in over the school section, and that's not Indian land, out that way, not till you've gone six, eight miles. All right. Now for awhile, it's all smooth going there, rolling prairie, like, no rocks, no trees, no anything. There could be gold there, sure, but who'd know where to look for it? Miners look for gold where two kinds of rocks come together. You know that?"

"We do now," Hostetter said.

"The malapie!" Shurtz said. "The lava beds out on the reservation!" He raised his arms like a senator unveiling a statue, "Lots of rocks, lots of broken country—and if you can believe what you hear, lots of hideouts for fellas the law's lookin' for one place or another."

Wellman said at once: "I don't want to end up like those men in that wagon."

"All right," Shurtz said. "Not now. I don't want to get killed, neither. But if the Army comes in, or U.S. Marshals, if the reservation's opened to claims and settlements—we're in it together, the three of us. We claim on the malapie, first."

Hostetter slowly nodded, and the three men shook hands.

* * * *

The only customer in the store when Sydnor got there was an Indian, one of the lower members of the tribe, a man they called Blanket Moe whose reservation seemed to be on Sydnor's porch. Someone had given him a dime, and he was buying a bottle of citrate of magnesia with it; the favorite drink of the town's Indians, a circumstance that Dr. Arnall had frequently threatened to write up for the Journal of American Medicine.

Sydnor grunted at him, and Blanket Moe shuffled back out to the porch and his favorite post, leaning near the door begging for change and candy.

"Much business, Ellen?"

The girl said: "Quite a bit, Mr. Sydnor."

Sydnor grunted again, and went over to the cash box. He lifted the bunch of sales slips Ellen had made out in his absence, lifted them as though they had personally insulted him. He started at the bottom, looking for a running story on how his store had done in his hour's absence.

"What's this, what's this? Forty dollar's worth of goods charged to the county? Who's going to pay it, Ellen?"

Ellen Lea's voice was patient; there weren't many jobs for women in Rock Spring. "Jack Romayne charged those, Mr. Sydnor. Groceries for his trip."

Sydnor said: "He had no right. He gets a salary from the county. That's plenty."

Ellen Lea said, demurely: "I could hardly stop him, Mr. Sydnor. An armed man, and an officer of the law!"

"You could have sent for me!"

"He said he'd just come from you, and naturally, I thought you'd told him…"

"I'd done no such thing," Sydnor said, but his tone was milder. He was looking over the other slips. "Quite a run on the hardware department," he said. "See where Nat Palmer bought a shovel and a pick. Maybe he's going to fix the walk in front of his house after all. Another pick for Woodward. Brister bought a three pound hammer. Picks for Glidden and Patten, and a shovel for…"

He slammed his hand down on the slips, suddenly getting a picture from the purchases. "Those idiots," he said. "Want to get themselves scalped. Doc Beals should have kept his mouth shut. News of the gold strike's all over town."

Ellen Lea said nothing for a moment. Then she said: "Maybe they're not going out now. Maybe they're just buying the tools so they'll be sure to have them when it's safe on the prairie."

Sydnor turned his huge bulk to stare at her. "Would have thought of that myself in a minute." He stamped over to the hardware part of the store, bent down. From his vest pocket he took a pencil, began working on the price tags, wheezing slightly.

Lize Fisher came in from the street, said: "Hi, Miz' Lea," and went straight to the hardware corner, hefted a shovel and then picked up the price tag, read it in the light from the front door. "Twenty dollars for a shovel. Man, they's something wrong here, Charley, mighty wrong."

Charley Sydnor said: "Take it or leave it. You can pay Ellen there."

Lize Fisher went across to Ellen, pulled out his wallet, untied the end and counted out the greenbacks. Then he stamped out of the store.

Sydnor came as dose to laughing as he ever did. "Good work, Ellen," he said. The shovel had been three dollars and a half a few minutes before. "You finish changing those tags, now. I'm going home to lunch."

When he passed the sheriff's office, Wellman was in the door. "Hey, Charley, you've got the keys to this place. I want to lock up. I got some bookkeeping and so on to do over at the Great Chance."

"You're going out on the prairie," Sydnor said. "You're going gold hunting and get yourself scalped. I thought you had more sense, Wellman!"

"Well, no," Wellman said. His deference slipped a little and his voice flared. "But maybe I would, if I could leave the business. But my poker dealer quit on me, rode off with Jack Romayne, and I'm looking for another. There's three, four men I want to see, Lee Patten, if he's sober and…"

"He's probably gone," Sydnor said. "Bought gold digging tools in my store."

Wellman said: "Well, you can't blame him, Charley. A man who wouldn't risk his life to get rich maybe deserves to die poor. But I've got to find a poker dealer."

"If you change your mind," Sydnor said, "I'll be glad to sell you a shovel."

Wellman smiled politely, and Sydnor was free to go on to

his house. He was very hungry, with a heavy man's hunger; his body didn't want food, it demanded it, furiously and with anger.

He walked faster.

When he opened the front door of his house he could smell the fine smell of onions frying, and his stomach surged with relief. He hung up his hat and walked fast into the dining room. This house didn't shake with his heavy stride.

From the kitchen Phyllis' voice called: "It'll be ready in a minute. Liver and onions, canned tomatoes with bread in them; baked potato with cheese, hot biscuits. For dessert I made floating island."

This was the routine of their noons. Next to making money he liked to eat, and next to eating he liked to talk about food, to hear about it.

Down at the store Ellen Lea finished changing the price tags and spread her lunch on the back counter. Two sandwiches—slightly gritty from being exposed to Rock Spring's climate all morning—a piece of cake and a pickle.

X

By drumming his heels hard on the white horse's side, Dan Younge got up alongside the lieutenant. "I don't know whether you noticed, Beer." He pointed a long finger. "That isn't smoke and it isn't rain coming up."

"It's dust," the lieutenant said. "I noticed a long time ago."

"Indians?"

"Could be."

Behind them, Rylan was passing the word to the troopers to check their guns. The white horse began lagging again, and Dan drummed at his ribs, but started falling back anyway. The lieutenant turned his head. "Do you speak Shoshone, Younge?"

"Hell, no," Dan Younge said. "Do you, Beer? You know that's a tantalizing name you got, out here on the dusty prairie."

"I never thought of it. No, I don't speak any of the Indian tongues. I had some Spanish at the Academy, but I guess we are too far north for the Indians to speak Spanish."

Rylan passed a quiet order, and one of the troopers turned out of column and dismounted. The one who had been clinging to a stirrup mounted quickly, sighing: "I never thought a McClellan would feel like my old grandmother's lap to me." He trotted back into column with the new runner clinging to his stirrup.

Watching this, Dan Younge had let the slow-walking pack horse pick his own gait again, and he was moving back along the column. Rylan called to him: "Stay somewhere around the middle of the column, Mr. Younge. Alongside the sheriff."

"All right, sarge."

Satisfied that he had other horses to follow, the pack horse kept up now, went in alongside Jack Romayne as Dan Younge swung the hackamore. "How you doing, Jack?"

The sheriff sat up on his high troop horse, shoulders bent, taking the shock off his creased and tied up ribs. "Is that another column of troops we're meeting?"

"Shoshone, the lieutenant thinks."

Romayne said: "Ah," and was silent a moment. "Well, if they are Indians we may find out what we came out here to find out."

"Yeah. You speak Indian? The officer was asking."

"No," Jack Romayne said. "About three words, all of them dirty. Dan?"

The dust cloud was coming closer. The two lines of travel would meet in a few minutes. Dan Younge watched, and automatically felt for his rifle under his leg, the rifle Romayne had brought from the sheriff's office. But Romayne was saying his name again, and he turned his head and said: "Yeah?"

"You don't have much use for me anymore, do you?"

Dan Younge said: "It's customary for gamblers and sheriffs not to get along."

The hand holding the Army reins beat on the hollow pommel of the saddle. "That is not so. It's just not so, Dan. We always got along fine, you and I. We were getting along-fine when I got shot. Then you figure I went yellow."

"It could happen to anybody. Shock. Surprise."

"Yes, it could. Till something like this hits you, you don't know what it's like. I…"

"Forget it, kid. I'll keep my mouth shut back in Rock Spring. If we' ever get there. Here come your little red brothers."

It was only from a distance that the prairie looked flat. It was level only as a rough sea is level; nearby it would rise to smooth topped heights higher than a man's head, but from one height to another the hollows disappeared in the near distance.

Lieutenant Beer, trying to get a wounded man back to Rock Spring, had kept his patrol along a hollow. The Shoshone had been following another.

Now the two shallow canyons came together, and the lieutenant was face to face with the Indians.

There were a slew of them, Dan Younge realized. More Indians than he had ever seen together, even at beef issue time on reservations. More Shoshone than Rock Spring thought lived on the whole reservation.

The lieutenant up ahead had pulled his column to a halt, had raised his hand in the traditional gesture of goodwill to the first of the Shoshone. The Indians were coming to a shuffling, disordered halt themselves, and as the dust settled and the Shoshone fanned out, Dan Younge saw that there were women and children in the mob, and the sight made him breathe easier.

Not that there weren't still twenty or thirty braves to each soldier, but the Indian men were not on the warpath.

But they might be when they saw where the patrol was.

The Indian leader on the right of a group of three said; "I speak English. Pretty good English."

Dan Younge eyed the man more closely. He was as dark as any of the Shoshone, but his hair was cut short above the collar of his coyote skin jacket, and his features lacked the clear definition of the Indian. Probably a half breed, or maybe less. Maybe just plain squaw man.

The lieutenant said: "Good. You will tell your people what I say. We are on our way to Rock Spring. Behind, in our party, is the sheriff of Rock Spring. Some men were killed, out here on the reservation. The sheriff was looking for the killers; somebody shot him. We are taking him back to Rock Spring."

The interpreter grunted. He said: "I'll tell him all that, lieutenant. Sho. And then he'll say what's that to the Shoshone? They didn't kill nobody."

Lieutenant Beer said: "I haven't said they have. On the other hand, the Indian agent, Major Miles, has sent for troops. He may know something."

The interpreter nodded again. Unexpectedly he said: "I'm Nate Allen," and then turned to the two old men with him. He talked awhile and then waited. The old man in the middle talked awhile too, and then the old man on the left. Nate Allen gave his grunt again, and said some more in the strange tongue. Both old men shrugged.

Nate Allen said: "Lieutenant, I told 'em all you had to say. They're going to Rock Spring, too, to see Miles. They're mad. Men are on the reservation, men who got no right there. Mining men. Some of the people have been killed. They say…" He broke off.

Beer's voice was sharp: "Yes, go on, what do they say?"

"They say if you're such a hell of a soldier, go get the men who killed our people. I told 'em you wouldn't like it, but they don't seem to care."

Beer grinned, and one of the old men chuckled, wickedly. Then the lieutenant's face sobered. "One of your people, Allen? You're no Indian."

"I'm quarter breed."

The lieutenant said: "If the agent asks me to, I'll do my best to rid the reservation of trespassers." Some of the young bucks huddling their ponies up behind the leaders were grumbling, there was a lifting of rifles and knives.

Nate Allen stared at the army officer from under his dark brows. He was frowning now. He said clearly and coldly, "Sometimes I think half the troubles of the West could get themselves solved if they'd shut up that school at West Point," and then he turned and talked in the Indian tongue awhile, and when he finished both old men were frowning, too.

This time only the old man in the middle answered. The other one merely nodded his head.

Nate Allen said: "Two Eagles says it was always this way. They have tried to do what the white men wanted, what the guv'ment wanted. In return, Washington sends 'em men like you and Major Miles. Take off, now, soldier. Git them…trespassers today."

Lieutenant Beer said harshly: "I'll run my patrol my own way."

Nate Allen said: "You fool! Git outa here! Git to Miles, tell him how many we are, how mad we are. Try and get some sense into his fat head."

Lieutenant Beer was breathing hard now. But his voice was controlled and firm and he turned to Sergeant Rylan and gave his order. "Column left, march."

When Rylan raised his arm to give the signal, several of the young Shoshones brought their rifles up. But when they saw the troops were moving out, they held their fire.

Lieutenant Beer marched his men along the massed front of the Indian mob before making another left turn and heading for Rock Spring. It took him two or three minutes to pass all the Indians, though the troop horses were fast walkers.

It was not much of a show of strength.

Then the column moved across the prairie at a trot, Jack Romayne cursing as he rode.

The Shoshone were soon left behind.

XI

Wellman, Shurtz and Hostetter, those sachems of Rock Spring, had made a survey. Twelve men had left town, moved out by the rumor of gold. Remaining were a hundred and fourteen reasonably able-bodied men, ninety-odd women and some kids.

This was reinforced, presently, by two ranch families, three men and a nearly grown boy, plus women and children. Somebody had shot at them as they worked their fields. No dead, no wounded, but they took it as fair warning and skedaddled for town.

They demanded action, and sheriff action. Since Sydnor was acting sheriff, with Wellman as his almost legal deputy, they got a promise that Jack Romayne would look after them as soon as he returned, if he did.

The farmers screamed loudly of taxes paid and services not received, of writing to the State Legislature, to Washington, to heaven itself. Then they settled down near the big spring to await the sheriff.

Afternoon was wearing out when a rancher's kid, name of Gresham, larruped into town on a pretty good cutting pony, flinging himself off in front of the sheriff's office, pounding on the locked door, his eyes too bloodshot to read the notice telling him to come to Sydnor's store.

Behind him the cutting horse stood, untied, head down, wetting the dusty street with the sweat that poured off his belly.

Shurtz came out of his hotel and went across the street to the sheriff's office. "Here, boy," he said. "That's no way to treat a good horse! He'll get the heaves, standing hot that way in the wind."

Young Gresham turned and spread eagled himself against

the office door, heaving almost as much as the horse. "Where's the sheriff, old man?"

"Here," Shurtz said. "A little respect, youngster! The sheriff's out of town. Can't you read?"

The kid's face fell apart all at once. It was like the sheriff had been the end of a crusade for him; like the touch of sheriff-hand or the sight of sheriff-face was needed to stop the march of some fatal disease through his body, and now, denied it, he was resigned to die.

Shurtz said: "What is it, boy?"

A half dozen of Rock Spring's finest loafers had drifted over to see what went on, and with them Hostetter, from his feed store. He said to Shurtz: "What is it, Al?"

Shurtz shook his head. "Boy's been kicked by a mule and lost his senses."

The Gresham boy got his wind back, then. "They killed Paw," he said. "He was out riding fence, and they killed him. Tied him on his hoss, an' he come home thataway. An' they follered him, and Maw went for the shotgun, an' they…they…"

Shurtz said sharply: "They killed your mother, too?"

The boy nodded.

Hostetter said: "Indians? Shoshone?"

The Gresham boy shook his head.

There was a lot of silence there in the street of Rock Spring. Somebody said that they ought to send for Charley Sydnor, but nobody moved, though surely all had seen a crying boy before.

What they would have done next is hard to say; because a new diversion broke them away from the Gresham boy. One of the farm kids climbed the big rock, and from up there had seen something; he was yelling and waving his arms.

His father climbed up with him, and his deeper voice boomed down the canyon of the street. "Soldiers. Hey, folks, the Army's got here at last."

And so the whole of Rock Spring was lined up to see Lieutenant Beer bring his column into town, the handful of yellow legs and Jack Romayne and Dan Younge.

Health flowed back into the community. The Army was here, the Army would protect them.

Beer dismounted, handed his reins to his orderly, turned to Rylan. "Sergeant, find a flat place to camp, requisition fodder for the horses, free meat for the men if you can and keep everyone together."

He looked down the line. Several of his troopers were licking their lips. He said: "All right, Rylan. Pick a man you can trust, and tell him to go get enough beer to fill each man's canteen cup once. Here." He reached in his pocket, took out a couple of greenbacks and handed them over. "But no more."

Dan Younge had helped Jack Romayne off his troop horse; its regular rider scrambled into the saddle at once. Dan waited, but Jack Romayne said nothing, and finally the gambler told the soldiers, "Thanks a lot," and moved away to the sheriff's office. Lieutenant Beer, behind them, was asking to be directed to the Indian agent.

Romayne had fumbled the key out of his vest pocket, was unlocking the office door. "Extra key," he said. "I always carry it."

Dan Younge said nothing until they were inside the office. Then he said: "Thanks for the use of the packhorse, Romayne."

Jack Romayne said: "You think I'm yellow. It's a thing could have happened to any man. Shock. Surprise."

Dan Younge said:

"If I told your good people about you, maybe they'd fire you and make me sheriff. I don't want to be."

He turned and went back out on the street, poorer by a saddle and a bridle and a horse than he had been when last he walked Rock Spring. He went down the board sidewalk and into the Great Chance, and Wellman, from behind the bar, said: "So you came back."

"No other place to go. Give me a whiskey."

Wellman tapped a bartender's shoulder, said: "On the

house," and then, "You'll work tonight, Dan?"

Dan Younge said: "Sure. I'm dead broke. I'll make money for you tonight, there's soldiers in town, fresh money. And a sergeant and an officer… Also, there's about a million Indians, more or less, about to descend on the town. But I don't think they're here to gamble."

Wellman's mouth fell open. "What—what—?"

"A lot of their people have been killed. Being good, law-abiding Indians, they are coming here to ask Miles to order the soldiers to run down the killers."

"They can't do that," Wellman cried. "Those soldiers are all we've got between us and…"

"And what?" Dan asked. He tapped his whiskey glass and the bartender filled it again, slid him a bowl of pretzels.

He sat there. Sydnor came in, then Hostetter, Miles, the lieutenant and Jack Romayne, with a fresh bandage from Dr. Arnall. They held their conference at the bar, the biggest room in town.

Lieutenant Beer said: "I sent a corporal to take word to the fort, tell them where I've gone. They'll relieve us, I'm sure."

"They'd better," Major Miles said. "Those Indians are likely to lay siege to the town. They—well not Shoshone, but Cheyenne—did that once before, up north."

Dan Younge moved to the baize-covered table and picked up a deck of cards. A couple of heads turned his way; the lure of gambling never died, and a good poker dealer could always make out.

Shurtz said: "The Gresham boy said the leader of the gang that killed his folks wore a big, floppy white hat. Any of you place that?"

Nobody answered him. Two men drifted to Dan's table and then another and he reached in his drawer and laid out a fresh pack, nodded to one of the men to break the seal. Another man was coming to join them.

There had been no answer to Shurtz's question, no great interest in trying to answer it.

Yet, that was the first time White Hat was mentioned in Rock Spring. There would be plenty more times.

XII

Over his player's heads Dan saw the swinging doors slam open with enough force to almost keep them that way. Wellman stumbled in, still holding the halter rope he'd taken to go after a cow a townsman had lost over Dan's table. "Indians," he yelled. "Right on the edge of town."

Dan was dealing to three men—two soldiers and a townsman. Corporal Sully said: "Hit me once, and then me an' Penroyal better git back to camp."

Dan dealt him a king, put a three and then a five on Penroyal's cards, dealt the townsman, Jensen, out. He handed himself a twenty and collected. "Indians are not much for night moving," he said. "These must be in a hurry."

"They smell the blood of a cavalryman," Sully said, unexpectedly. "I wish I'd stayed in Boston." But he moved through the crowded barroom with a swagger, pulling on his big gauntlets as he went, followed by the young Penroyal.

Dan Younge looked at Jensen, and shrugged. "Game's closed," he said.

But the bar wasn't. The men of Rock Springs were pushing up to it, buying courage at so much—too much—an ounce. A man could almost tell how much an individual had drunk by the force and eloquence of his boasts.

There was no use trying to deal till the excitement bubbled down a little.

He said good night to Wellman, but the owner never heard him. However, Big Red, the head bartender, caught Dan's eye, and said: "I'll tell him," without stopping the rapid bottle and glass work of his hands.

Dan Younge passed out into the street. Sober townsmen elbowed him in their anxiety to get inside and correct that condition; the news had gone up and down canyon in a hurry.

Here came Sydnor, preceded by his belly. Dan Younge, starting to take his usual pre-bed stroll, decided to go down canyon; it seemed politic to avoid the vicinity of Sydnor and Phyllis Sydnor's house.

There was a lamp burning in the sheriff's office, and that was another place he was not anxious to visit. But Jack Romayne was in the doorway; he called: "Younge? That you, Dan?"

Dan Younge sighed and moved towards the sheriff. "Yeah."

The sheriff smiled. "You got posse money due you. Three dollars a day and twenty cents a mile. We must have covered—what—fifty, sixty miles."

Dan Younge said: "Sydnor'd never pay it; and it's not enough to make me fight him. And—not meaning to tell you your business—there's trouble downtown—the kind that flows gently from a bottle."

"I'll get down there," Jack Romayne said. "There's a woman coming. Prob'ly somebody wants me to haul her spouse out of Wellman's."

But it was Ellen Lea. She stood in the light from the office, and said: "Oh, Jack. Saw your light. I'm not exactly a shrinking violet, but I'd appreciate a sober escort home."

Jack Romayne said: "Dan was just telling me that Rock Spring seems to be drowning itself tonight. Work to do. Will you wait, Ellen, unless Dan Younge here..." He let the question go unsaid.

Dan Younge said: "A pleasure," because there was nothing else to say.

Ellen Lea said: "Oh, I'd not take you out of your way, Mr. Younge, Jack..."

But Romayne was already gone down the sidewalk, towards the trouble. Dan Younge watched him go and thought, wound and all, he heads for the trouble he's used to; it's the unknown that frightens him. He said: "I always take a walk before bed," and held out his arm to Ellen Lea.

She took it, letting her fingers rest lightly on his bent arm, and said: "I've heard and seen you on those walks, Mr. Younge, and wondered. A widow sleeps lightly."

This was a subject to be avoided. "So does a gambler."

Ellen Lea said: "It must be lonesome, being the only professional gambler in a town."

When a lady used the word lonesome, Dan Younge shied; towards, if she were married, away if she was not. He said: "Well, a gambler's hours are good, and I get the exercise I need horseback riding. Which reminds me; I need to buy a horse. Do you know anybody with a good one for sale?"

They were halfway between downtown and Sydnor's now. She said, "This is my place. I'll ask around about a horse, Mr. Younge. Most news passes through the store every day."

She had left a lamp burning in her window, she must have gone home to supper and then back down to Sydnor's store. He didn't envy her working conditions. It was past one o'clock, and Charley Sydnor would probably expect her to open the store at seven tomorrow. Or maybe be there earlier to dust.

Under the circumstances, he could hardly blame her for looking for a husband, even a professional gambler.

His sense of humor got the better of him then, and he began to chuckle softly as he turned back downtown. Wait till you're asked, Danny Boy. There's something between her and Jack Romayne, and a good, steady sheriff's a nice prospect.

XIII

Jack Romayne woke up the next morning and knew, as a man does, that his wound was on the mend. Since he had broken up three fights the night before, this was pretty good. And in a way, it was bad, too. If the bullet crease had turned into something serious, it would have vindicated him in Dan Younge's eyes.

He shaved carefully, because he intended to consult Lieutenant Beer, and he had an idea that a neat and soldierly appearance would help him.

He found the officer in front of the hotel, quietly watching the street traffic. He said: "You heard about the Indians? I plan to get up a posse of citizens, ride out to the Shoshone camp, show them the men of Rock Spring are under arms and ready to ride with your troops."

"Troops is a mighty poor description for a depleted platoon," Beer said. He pulled at his smooth shaven chin. "Call my command a squad, and I wouldn't get insulted. Sheriff, you may have an idea. It would depend on how much control you can hold over your citizens. One hothead could start an Indian war."

"That's the chance we have to take," Jack Romayne said.

Lieutenant Beer said: "Every time I hear someone use that phrase, I know he hasn't thought out the thing he plans to do."

Jack Romayne said: "Lieutenant, I can be pushed a little too far. I suggest we go see Major Miles."

"A third man seems indicated."

A little knot of townsmen had collected around them; but the two officials, Army and civilian, spoke in low voices, and nobody ventured close enough to overhear. Now, as Romayne and Beer started for their horses, the curiosity seekers followed them.

Beer said: "Rock Spring seems to have declared a legal holiday."

Jack Romayne was mounting, a little clumsily, the action pulled at the half-healed crease on his side. He didn't answer.

They pulled out of the hitching rail and turned towards the Indian Agency. It was out of town, slightly, on the edge of the reservation land about a third of the way to the Shoshone camp that made itself evident this clear and windless morning by the smoke from a hundred campfires.

"They don't look like a war party," Jack Romayne said.

"Wouldn't know," Lieutenant Beer said. "Haven't seen many."

The sheriff laughed in his easy manner. "To tell you the truth, I've never seen any. Cowboying around, I always avoid hostile country."

Beer said: "Lucky."

"I thought it was smart."

The high gate of the Agency was unmanned, but the flag was flying, indicating that the government was in operation. Inside the board building, opposite the big Agency store, a male secretary said, "Good morning, gentlemen. Major Miles is in his office. I'll see if he can see you."

Jack Romayne laughed, but Lieutenant Beer said: "Certainly."

The clerk went through a painted wooden door and closed it behind him. Beer said: "Sheriff, never disturb the even tenor of a red taper's day. What's a minute, more or less?"

The penpusher came back and bowed. "Major Miles will see Lieutenant Beer and Sheriff Romayne."

"Nice of him," Jack Romayne said, and followed the Army man into the sacred inner office of the Indian agent.

Major Miles came from behind his desk, a cheerful looking man, neat in a black suit and white shirt. He held out a well scrubbed hand. "Sheriff, Lieutenant, I was just about to walk into town to look for you."

"We rode out," Jade Romayne said.

"Quite so. In this job, I'm at a desk so much, I walk when I get a chance." He laughed and patted his slightly plump belly. "Well, well. I gather the problem is, what to do and who's to do it?"

Lieutenant Beer said: "On reservation land, in reservation matters, I am to be at the disposal of any Indian Bureau official who cares to take the responsibility."

The sheriff said: "Short and to the point: I want to assemble a posse—a large posse—of townsmen, and take them out, with Lieutenant Beer's men, to see the Indians."

Miles shot a quick look at Beer. "Armed men?" he asked. "On the reservation?"

Jack Romayne said: "If there's going to be a fight, I don't think Rock Spring ought to have it where the women and children are. If there isn't going to be a fight, your Indians aren't going to be hurt by the sight of men carrying guns."

Major Miles nodded. "Very well put. And yet… Let's hear from the Army."

Beer smiled slightly. "Those Indians say their people have been murdered, including some women. No use my talking to them again; I'm under the orders of your Bureau."

Miles said, slowly: "Let's leave it at this. I'll go parley with the Indians, and Lieutenant Beer will provide me with some of his men, few enough so that the Shoshone will not take alarm. Sheriff Romayne will come with us or not, as he sees fit, and he'll make every effort to keep his townspeople away."

"Good," Beer said. He put out his hand and he and Miles shook, then they both shook hands with the sheriff. Beer said, "I'll be back in half an hour. I want to make sure my men are properly turned out. I understand Indians are strong on ceremony."

XIV

Dan Younge had awakened at his usual hour. Now, at eleven, he came to the door of the hotel, lit a cigar, and leaned there, smoking, looking out over the main street.

There was a clatter and a cloud of dust, and the lieutenant rode by, all in blue and spotless yellow, followed by eight of his men, as well-groomed as he. They rode at stiff attention, eyes forward, backs arched, and one of the men carried a guidon and another an American flag.

Before the cavalry dust had settled, the men in the crowd began talking it up, each in his own way. Some muttered and some yelled, but the result was the steady hum that any man knows—too well—if he has ever heard a mob about to form.

Dan Younge blew a smoke ring. It hung on the air.

Jack Romayne came out of his office, badge catching the bright sun, gun slung alertly on his hip, hat tilted back to show his pleasant face.

A man called out: "The Army just rode by, dressed fit to kill, goin' to call on them Injuns fer afternoon tea."

Wellman was shoving through the crowd, and behind him Sydnor. They ranged themselves in front of Romayne, forcing him back a little into the office. Dan Younge grinned to himself. The real bosses of Rock Spring talked to the sheriff in voices too low for the crowd and Dan Younge to hear. Now Wellman was turning and facing the crowd, but from his attitude, and from the bulk of Sydnor behind him, it was the storekeeper's decision that was being relayed.

"You're taxpayers and citizens," Wellman said. Behind him Sydnor's lips moved. Wellman nodded and went on. "The sheriff agrees that it might be a good idea for you men to be standing by."

The men scrambled for their horses. Romayne was already mounted and riding out. Sydnor made no move to go, nor Wellman, and no doubt Shurtz and Hostetter were staying home, too. The street boiled with dust.

Wellman came over to Dan Younge. "Glad to see you're not riding. I wouldn't want to lose my gambler."

"Your interest touches my heart, Mr. Wellman. Love me enough to stand for a beer?"

"A good idea, Younge."

The big bartender drew them two, and one for himself. "We only got three kegs of beer left, Mr. Wellman. Somebody better get the trails open soon."

"Until they are open, beer'll be four bits a glass," Wellman said. "Dan, how'll the blockade affect your table?"

Dan Younge shrugged. "When money can't get out of a place," he said, "the house percentage will start eating it up, I suppose. Of course, there are quite a few men in town who don't gamble, and an awful lot more whose wives are going to get pretty mad if we start doing too well. They might try and get an ordinance against gambling."

"We'll cross that bridge when…" Wellman broke off. Horses were drumming down the street and not from the direction of the reservation.

"Can't be the men coming back," the bartender said.

But Dan Younge was already in the door. Wellman crowded him. These were not townsmen that rode Rock Spring; they were a ragged bunch, with the flat hats and jack-eared boots of miners.

The leader's hat was white and hugely-brimmed. Seeing the men in the saloon door, he pulled his horse up, and while the animal was still rearing, snatched a gun from his hip and fired.

Wellman ducked back into the saloon, and Dan Younge dropped to one knee. The shot flicked splinters from the door-frame.

Dan Younge said: "Red, lemme have the shotgun."

The barman must have passed it to Wellman. It came under Dan Younge's arm, and he threw it up, fired without taking much aim. The middle of the street was pretty far range for a sawed-off bar gun, the shotgun was meant to foil holdups, not to hunt rabbits with.

The shot must have tickled White Hat's horse. He danced, and the big man on his back rocked perilously in his saddle. He fired again, the shot going high, and then galloped on down the street, his men coming up after him. As they passed the sheriff's office, now deserted, they shot out the glass window that had a sheriff's star in it. Going by the store, they caused Charley Sydnor to tumble back into its dark depths with a lack of dignity unusual in the town's richest man.

"Now you know," Dan Younge said. He stood up, handed the shotgun to Wellman. "Miners. They must have been hiding out in the malapie. They'll be back. They need supplies."

Wellman said: "Well, damn it, a saloon's what they'll head for. I... They must have been watching, must have seen the men leave town."

Dan Younge said, "They'll be back. There's a half dozen soldiers up by the big rock, the noise'll bring 'em down. Till then, you and Red can hold them off. I'm going over to the store."

"Sydnor..."

Dan Younge said: "To hell with Sydnor," and ran across the street into the store. Sydnor was cramming shells into a double barrelled shotgun. Ellen Lea was back against the till. Dan Younge said: "Give me a six shooter, Mrs. Lea. And then start loading all the rest of the ones in stock. Stay back of the counter there, and throw them to me as they're ready:"

There was a flour barrel and a sugar barrel and a pickle keg. He rolled the keg into the doorway, backed it up with the sugar barrel, and had to leave the flour barrel alone because the hoofs had drummed back.

He was behind the sugar barrel, crouched down, when

White Hat pulled up in front of the store. There were only ten or twelve men with him. Dan Younge grinned at himself; they had seemed like an army when they went by the Great Chance shooting at him.

White Hat roared, "We're starvin' men, and we know they's only a handful of you in town. If you don't want your houses burned and your womenfolk killed, start throwin' out some edibles."

Sydnor's answering roar was characteristic. "If you're who we think you are, you have gold to pay for what you want."

"We're wanted for murder," White Hat said. "It ain't gonna hurt us to be sheriffed after over some stolen groceries. Throw 'em out! We need bacon an' flour, an' salt. We need coffee an'…"

Dan Younge fired. As he did so, something nudged his leg. He almost turned, then remembered, and dropped his left hand down. It was a loaded six shooter. Another arrived before he could raise his hand—Ellen Lea was getting practiced at loading.

He couldn't tell if his bullet did any good, but with unlimited ammunition and no need to stop to load, he ought to be able to stop the outlaw miner problem before it got a fair start.

Red was booming away with the shotgun, and then men in the street were firing back. Suddenly the pickle barrel burst wide open, and taught Dan Younge that pickles make poor cover. He was drenched with the brine, and blinded by it.

He scrubbed at his eyes with his neat black sleeve, and when he could see again the scene in the street had changed. The miners were gone, and the last of Sergeant Rylan's tiny garrison was disappearing after them.

Dan Younge stood up, and turned to Ellen Lea. "Hardly a hero. I must smell like a pickling works."

She said: "With dill seeds in your hair instead of laurels," and, defiant of Sydnor, threw him a brand new huckaback towel out of stock.

He scrubbed at his face and coat with it, chuckling over her remark. It showed an education and a point of view that he hadn't expected in Rock Spring.

Sydnor, grunting and red in the face, was wheeling the sugar out of danger of being contaminated with the free-flowing pickle brine. Dan Younge dropped the towel on the floor, and then picked it up again, realizing that if he didn't, Sydnor would make Ellen do it. He said: "They won't be back. They must have thought all the soldiers went off to the Indian parley."

"You're a cool one," Sydnor said. "Ever think of giving up gambling?"

"For what?"

"This town could use a law officer who was around sometimes when he was needed."

"I'm too fond of money for work like that," Dan Younge said. "I was drinking a beer when this started; think I'll go finish it. The troops won't catch White Hat. Their horses are too big to be very fast.

Sydnor cleared his throat. "Yes," he said. "And those miners surely headed for the malapie. Pretty broken country in there for a big horse. You ever seen it?"

"Closest I've ever been was a couple of miles, when I was out with Romayne."

"Romayne," Sydnor grunted. "That one's a lot of use to Rock Spring."

Ellen Lea said sharply: "He thought the danger was from the Indians, and he went out to meet it."

Sydnor looked astounded.

He said: "Well, maybe," and went back into the store.

She's serious about Jack Romayne, Dan Younge thought. Too bad, nice girl. He bowed to her, and said, "Mrs. Lea, you and I make a good team in a gunfight," and went out in the street, back to his beer.

XV

Lieutenant Beer said: "You can promise these Indians justice, but you cannot promise them that I'll lead my squad of men into country such as this malapie you are talking about. I'm sorry!" and then was silent as Nate Allen translated to the two chiefs. The one called Ironhand started shaking his head dolefully.

But the older man was suddenly talkative. His speech flowed fast, his hands waved, he rolled in his saddle with the passion of what he had to say.

Jack Romayne found himself listening intently, though there was no possibility of understanding a word.

When the old man finished, he settled down in his raw wooden saddle again, and waited. It was impossible to believe that a moment before he had been so active.

Nate Allen shrugged, and looked from one to the other of the three white men. "Two Eagles says he doesn't blame the soldiers for not wanting to go into the malapie after the killers. It was not the soldiers' women that were killed, not their children. So, he says, give the Indians good rifles and good pistols, like the killers have, and the young men of the tribe'll go into the malapie, and get the killers themselves, and there will be peace on the prairie. That's what he says."

Jack Romayne shouted: "No! I got seventy-five, a hundred men over there, just over that rise. They got guns, and they'll use 'em before they let us arm the Indians. It's bad enough with the smooth bores an' old single shot pistols the Shoshone have now."

"We need our guns for hunting," Nate Allen said. "If yore folks didn't want to live next to Indians, they shouldn't have settled here first off."

Major Miles cried: "Gentlemen, gentlemen, we're not getting anyplace. I suggest…"

He broke off, and they all waited. And then he finished lamely, "I suggest we hold off all action till tomorrow, and hold another parley then."

The only trouble with the troops, Jack Romayne was thinking, is that there aren't enough of them. On the other hand, there are plenty of Rock Springers, but I can't get them organized into a posse. Maybe another man could; maybe Dan Younge could.

But he pushed the thought away and said, suddenly: "Lieutenant, would you ride with a posse if we had one?"

Lieutenant Beer looked startled. "I hadn't thought of that," he said. "Maybe I would. I can't think of anything against it; an officer is entitled to scout, if he wants to, and leave his command behind. Let me think it over."

Watching the soldiers, Jack Romayne hadn't heard riders coming up. The Indian chiefs and old Nate Allen were being crowded back, into safety, by young Indians who circled their ponies forward. Half of them were riding without saddles and hardly any of them had proper bridles, Romayne noticed, and the guns they carried were smooth bores and old single shot rifles—but there were a lot of them.

They made their ponies curvet and dance among the white men, separating Romayne from Beer, Beer from Miles. Beer passed a low order to his men: "Keep your hands away from your carbines; hold your reins high."

The riders, it became apparent in a moment, were a soldier and Dan Younge. The trooper made a sketchy salute. "From Sergeant Rylan, sir. Riders hit the town. We druv 'em off, but Schmidt an' Raikes is dead and Swite's wounded."

"Indians?"

"No, sir. White men. Miners. We wounded one, took him back to Rock Spring. He says they're fellas was run out of the Colorado diggings, sir."

Beer said: "All right. Fall in with the column, over there." He turned to Dan Younge. "Anything to add to that, Mr. Younge?"

Dan Younge said: "The men in town—Sydnor, Wellman and so on—want to beg you and Major Miles to settle with the Indians on any basis. I agreed to bring the word to you."

Beer said: "What everybody seems to want is for me and my men—and I've only got thirteen of them left—to ride into the malapie after these outlaws. That's the basis the Indians are willing to settle on. But the sheriff here has the idea that a few of my men and I go as scouts with a posse. That I'm willing to do." He turned in the saddle. "Mr. Allen!"

Seeing that there were only two of the gallopers, and that they had not come gun in hand, the braves had allowed their elders to come forward again.

Nate Allen said: "Yeah?"

Beer said: "You can hold your young men till—say—this time tomorrow?"

"Make it this afternoon. After dark, they might get to wardancing around the fires, and then they'd be out of hand. Make it before sundown today."

Beer stared at the half breed. "You're really out for peace," he said. "You're a good man, Mr. Allen."

"I'm a live one. Mean to stay so."

The words, the spoken wish, might have been a signal.

The townsmen, bored with waiting over the hill, had started passing bottles around. Now they were filled with courage, Great Chance brand; and they came over the rise and down on the parley hard.

Miles said quickly: "Stop them, Romayne."

But he didn't say how. Jack Romayne raised his reins, kicked back with his spurs, and the horse carried him forward till he was abreast of the men.

They split around Jack Romayne like water around a rock, and rode on for the Indians. Only a few of them carried rifles, but they all had six shooters, and maybe it was just some drunken fool trying to puncture the sky who fired the first shot.

But that did it. The warhoop that came up from the Indian braves might have come from one monstrous throat. The Indians rode into the townsmen with knives and clubs and the townsmen rode into the Shoshone with their guns out, and one horse screamed as its throat was cut.

Dust came up in a blinding, choking cloud, and Jack Romayne felt his horse taking him out of there. Suddenly there were Indian braves—last year's boys—on either side of him, and one of them grabbed his horse's bridle. The other grappled for Romayne's neck, trying to get a forearm under Jack Romayne's chin to pull his head back for the knife.

Jack Romayne felt pain go through his almost healed side. He got his gun out and fired—no need for aiming at that range—at the figure that held his bridle, felt the horse toss his head free.

He clubbed out with the gun and then was riding free, rolling in the saddle. He'd lost his stirrups but the horse was at a flat-bellied run, and it was easy to stay aboard.

All around him other men rode, and one of them, a man who'd driven wagon when the trails were open, a man named Walters, was crying: "We got run off. We got ourselves plain run off by a bunch of Indians." Tears ran down Walters' face, and it was a curious thing to see.

Bullet-noise could be heard behind them, and some of the men started lashing their horses with rein-ends and quirts; but the horses were already tired, and going as fast as they could.

Then Jack Romayne realized that no bullets whirred around them; the firing was not at them. He leaned back in his saddle and pulled the bit, and his horse stopped. The first thing he did was put his feet back in the covered stirrups.

There was another round of fire. It was regular and even. "That's the Army," Jack Romayne said. A few other men had pulled up, too.

He pulled his horse around, and started back for the scene of the battle, putting the horse to a stiff trot, standing in his stirrups to ease the shock. Three or four men came after him.

But before they got there, Lieutenant Beer came up out of a dip and stopped them with a raised palm. "The Shoshone have pulled deeper into the reservation," he said. "I dismounted my men and drove the Indians off with carbine fire."

"I came back as soon as I could round up some help," Jack Romayne said.

"Certainly," Beer said courteously. "Certainly. Sheriff, either you or I is Indian agent now, I'm not sure which. Major Miles was killed, the Indians got his body. I lost one of my men, too."

The officer gestured behind him. There was his little file of men, and one of them was belly down on his saddle, another trooper led his horse.

There was a civilian with the troops; Dan Younge had stayed to fight it out, alongside the military. Jack Romayne avoided the gambler's eyes.

Lieutenant Beer was still talking, and his voice was like that of a lonesome drunk. Jack Romayne, who had never seen a real gun fight before today had heard that they left men in a peculiar state of shock. "Twelve men," the officer said. "I have twelve men left. It's not exactly an Army."

Jack Romayne said: "I'm going to deputize every able-bodied man in town. That will make you up an army. We'll run them off, lieutenant."

"Who?" the officer asked, simply. "The miners or the Indians? Rock Spring has got itself pinched in a three-cornered war."

Romayne said: "I reckon that's right."

"I've got a good education," Beer said. "You know something about three-sided wars? It's impossible for anyone to win."

XVI

Sergeant Rylan's men had taken a prisoner. One of the troopers had shot a man off his horse, without killing him. The sergeant had brought him back to town, and Charley Sydnor, with his usual presence of mind, had invited the wounded man to his home and sent for Dr. Arnall.

Charley Sydnor waited in the drawing room of his big house. After awhile the doctor came out. He said: "We got the bullet out, Charley. He'll only be in bed a few days. That'll be two dollars."

Charley Sydnor grunted. The doctor shrugged and let himself out the front door.

Charley Sydnor slowly got to his feet. He patted his comfortable paunch, and made his ponderous way to the guest room door. He went in without knocking.

Phyllis was just propping the wounded miner up on three pillows.

Charley said: "I want to talk to this man, wife."

The miner had a wild, wary look in his eyes; the rest of his face was covered with a snarl of whiskers that made it impossible to place his age within ten years. He could have been forty or sixty.

Phyllis Sydnor quietly left the room.

Charley Sydnor said, "I'll call you Jonesy. Jonesy, you fellows have been hiding out in the malapie, haven't you?"

Jonesy said: "Out in that black rock country, yeah. We was headin' for the coast, and our hosses needed rest. They's grass and water in there."

Charley Sydnor let out a ponderous chuckle. "And gold," he said. Suddenly he moved across the room, snatched up the miner's clothes.

Jonesy yelled, "Put those down," and then groaned as the effort pulled at his wound.

But Sydnor went on searching. He found what he wanted in the hip pocket of Jonesy's woolen breeches—two thin pads of buckskin, nicely quilted. He went over to the bed, put the pokes in Jonesy's hands. "See, here's your gold. I'm your friend. Now, the doc says you'll be well soon."

"Said I chipped the top of my hip bone, smashed up my floatin' ribs some."

"Yeah," Sydnor said. "Now. Listen to me, Jonesy. I've treated you right. Took you in my home, got you a doctor, kept your goods safe for you."

Jonesy's eyes were cautious now. "Why?"

"Because I'm your friend," Sydnor said. "You go see that white-hatted leader of yours. Tell him there's a way into town under the big rock. I found it when I was building a storeroom. Tell him nobody with gold ever had to use a gun to do business with Charley Sydnor."

He took his big bulk to the door then and went out. He shouted: "Phyllis, where's my food? I gotta get back to the store!"

XVII

Ellen Lea was in trouble. Sydnor had left her alone in the store when Rylan's men brought the wounded outlaw in, and shortly thereafter she was swamped with visitors. It had begun to penetrate to the minds of Rock Spring that they were going to be townbound for quite awhile, and a natural desire to start hoarding food had grown out of this realization. But, having come to Sydnor's store to buy, they held back. Charley Sydnor had spent a busy night; not a price tag carried the same figures it had yesterday.

The men muttered and went away again. The women were more outspoken.

"Four dollars for a pound of coffee beans?" Mrs. Brister said. "Well, Mrs. Lea, you can just tell Charley Sydnor that I'm taking five pounds, and if there's more than the regular amount on my bill, he'll hear about it!"

"Mr. Sydnor said all charge accounts were closed. Everything's to be strict cash."

Several of the women began helping themselves to groceries. A man came to the counter and asked her for two boxes of .44 shells, and when he got them he deliberately put one in each pocket of his coat and, spitting on the floor, turned and walked out without paying.

Ellen Lea opened the till, got out a couple of pennies, and pushed through the profitless customers to the street.

There were small boys hanging around the livery stable, as usual. She gave two of them a penny each, and sent one up to the Sydnor house, the other to look for Jack Romayne.

On impulse she stopped Pat Patson, the blacksmith, who was angling across the street towards the Great Chance. "If Mr. Younge, the gambler, is in there, would you ask him to come over to Sydnor's store for a moment?"

Patson was shorter than she, a massive, bulky man, habitually unable to remove the coal dust from under his eyes. He cut his eyes at her now, cynically, and then shrugged. "Sure."

She turned back to the store. There goes my reputation, she thought. By tonight Rock Spring will have me sharing my bed with the gambler, by tomorrow I'll be bearing him twin babies out of wedlock.

That was a fool thing to do. And why in the world did I have to add "the gambler" after his name? Rock Spring isn't so big that Patson wouldn't have known which Dan Younge I meant.

By this time she was back at the door of the shop. She took a deep breath before entering its noisy interior; her reverie went on. I wonder how it feels to have people always put your trade after your name. Ellen Lea, the widow. I wouldn't like that. And a gambler is even more scorned than a widow. Charley Sydnor, the moneygrubber. Wellman, the saloonkeeper, Hostetter—

This wasn't doing her job. "Get out of here," she said. Her voice was surprisingly clear and loud. "Out of here, all of you. This store's closed till Mr. Sydnor gets here." She reached under the counter and got out the holdup pistol.

They left, fast. The predominantly female pack of customers—or robbers—went out of there, gabbling to each other, and she went across the floor after them, almost herding them, and then closed and locked the door.

She put the gun back, and sat down on the counter. Rock Spring really had something to talk about now! Someone was rapping at the door. She started to wave that the store was closed and then saw it was Dan Younge. She let him in and said, "Thanks for coming."

"What happened?"

"The customers were looting the place. Look at the price tags and you'll see why."

He looked and whistled. "You've got to admit Sydnor has nerve. Men have been lynched for not much more."

"I shouldn't have bothered you. I kind of lost my head, all of them screeching at me, yelling."

Dan Younge started building a cigarette. "Not your fault. You have to work and there aren't many things for a woman to do in Rock Spring."

She said: "Yes," and then shook her head. "No. I could take in washing."

"Too many doing that now," the gambler said. He split a match off a block from his pocket, struck it, waited for the sulphur to burn away, then lit his cigarette. His movements were very slow, very certain; it occurred to Ellen Lea that a woman could get a lot of comfort from hands like that. "No," Dan Younge said. "It's clerk in the store or catch you a husband… His lips clamped down. He smiled: "Or I could teach you to shill for me."

She said: "What's that?" Then at once she added: "Or should a lady know?"

"It's not all that bad. But a little too fancy for Rock Spring. Why, in the fancy gambling halls, San Francisco, Denver, they hire people to pretend to gamble, pretty girls, country-looking boys. The suck…the customers see them making money, think the table's having a bad night and hurry in to shower down."

"It sounds like nice work."

He shrugged. "As good as any. Nobody's really honest. Worked for a farmer one time. Twenty dollars a month, he said. End of the harvest, came to find out he had been charging me two bits a glass for milk. Food was thrown in, like he'd promised. So I owed him eight dollars for four months' work. And he went to church every Sunday, was on the board of the bank, he'd have fainted if you told him he was a crook."

"How old were you?"

Dan Younge said: "Fifteen." He laughed. "The life and times of Dan Younge. A book with a dog-eared cover. Your husband was a well-driller, wasn't he?"

Ellen Lea said: "Yes. We drove the drilling rig out from

Kansas on two wagons. It's in Glidden's barn, if you hear of anybody who'd like to buy it." She stood up from the counter. "Here's my boss."

After he'd been let in the front door, Sydnor went right to the point. "What is the store doing closed, in broad daylight, on a weekday?"

Ellen Lea said: "The new prices, Mr. Sydnor… Well, they seem…"

Sydnor brought a roar up from his ample belly. "There's been no mistake. I put those prices on there, and they stand! I pay you to take orders, not to decide policy!"

Dan Younge said: "Easy, mister, easy," in the tone a man uses to a horse. Sydnor kept on glaring at Ellen Lea.

"It wasn't I, Mr. Sydnor. The people got very angry. They started taking things without paying for them. One man took two boxes of cartridges, a man I'm not sure I know."

Sydnor grunted and turned on Dan Younge. "And you couldn't stop them?"

"I wasn't here," Dan Younge said quietly.

There was a note of warning in the gambler's voice, but Sydnor didn't seem to hear it. Incapable of telling an employee she had done the right thing—Ellen Lea might ask for a raise—he concentrated on Dan Younge. "See here, young fella. You seem capable, and you don't have much to do in the daytimes. I can pay you, not much, just to sit here, kinda keep order."

He got his answer promptly: "Certainly not."

Sydnor didn't get it. "You don't have to lift goods down from the shelf, wait on the customers. It's like picking money up in the street."

Dan Younge said: "And how small the coin, how deep the horse manure before you'd hesitate to do the picking?" He bowed to Ellen Lea. "Glad to be of assistance, ma'am." He left without bothering to close the front door.

Sydnor looked after him, genuinely puzzled. "Now, what's eating him?"

Ellen Lea had borrowed courage from the gambler. "I guess the same thing that's bothering the rest of the town. They don't think you ought to make money out of their troubles."

Sydnor had worn his hat down from the house, had never taken it off. He did so now, put on his long storekeeper's apron. He was frowning. "Why, that's what a man's in business for," he said slowly. "To buy cheap an' sell for all the market will stand. This is a monopoly, what I have here, a corner on the necessities market. A fella'd be a fool to pass it up. He might never get another chance."

Ellen Lea asked softly: "And being hated by everyone in town doesn't matter?"

Sydnor said simply: "Why, if I make the kind of money I expect, I'd be moving back East or maybe to California, wouldn't I? Who'd stay here when he'd made his pile?"

Ellen Lea shook her head and got ready for the customers; she got behind the counter and resolved to stay there. Sydnor himself went to stand in the door and let himself be seen by Rock Spring, an indication that trade was expected.

After awhile, he bellowed, "Romayne!" across the street.

The sheriff came to the door of the windowless office. Sydnor beckoned to him imperiously. Ellen Lea watched as Romayne crossed the street, and again the thought crossed her mind, Dan Younge wouldn't trot when Sydnor yelled.

Jack Romayne came in, with an easy smile for Ellen Lea, and a tighter, more careful one for Sydnor.

"Thought we were going to have some trouble here," Sydnor said. "Could have used you. But, like usual, you were someplace else. Now I got something for you to do for me."

"Anything," Jack Romayne said.

"G'wan up to my house, tell my wife to pack some clothes, get down here. There is getting to be a little feeling against me in this town. She an' I'll live back of the store for a while. Safer that way, with you across the street."

"Right away, Mr. Sydnor."

"An' I don't want to hear of you going off, gallivanting after any outlaws, any Indians. There's the Army for that. We need protection here in town, and we pay your salary."

Watching, Ellen Lea thought she saw Jack Romayne start to smile, and then suppress it. But that couldn't be. He couldn't be taking any pleasure out of the bullying the storekeeper was giving him. And from what she knew of men—they liked nothing better than what Sydnor called gallivanting.

No, she must have been wrong. That must have been chagrin and disappointment that she read in Jack Romayne's face, not happiness.

She smiled at him to ease the sting of Sydnor's boorishness, and he smiled back and then went away, up canyon towards Sydnor's house.

XVIII

At one o'clock in the morning, Dan Younge raised his hand and waved at Big Red, the bartender. Red promptly went to draw a beer; he knew the signal—the game was dosing. Carrying it himself he walked by Wellman who was leaning on the front of the bar keeping an eye on the customers.

Wellman elbowed away from the bar, followed Red over, and slouched down in one of the vacated chairs, idly watching his small gold mine. "Hear you were quite a hero out at the reservation today. And also at Sydnor's store."

Dan Younge's tone was sardonic. "I'm always a hero. And the reward—Sydnor asked me to be his floorwalker."

Wellman laughed. "When the trails open again, Sydnor had better be the first man out of town. I'm thinking of buying his store, when, as and if that happens. Want to run it for me?"

Dan Younge was genuinely surprised. He said: "Now, that's not anything I expected to hear. What's the connection between gambling and counterjumping?"

Wellman said flatly: "You're honest, you're smart and people like you."

Dan Younge said softly: "People like me as a gambler. They hate change. A gambler should stay a gambler."

"A lonesome life."

"I'm used to it." He looked up, saw Beer and Rylan coming towards the table, both of them in what he supposed was undress uniform, shirts open, forage caps on the back of their heads. "Table's closed, gentlemen."

"So are we," Beer said. "You cleaned our detachment out of available cash sometime back. I'd like to talk to you, Younge. We—Rylan and I—would like to talk to you. You're drinking beer?"

"I'll put the order in," Wellman said, rising. "I've got to circulate."

Beer and Rylan sat down simultaneously, and nothing marked the occasion more—the sergeant did not wait for his officer to be seated. They waited until the beer had been brought and the waiter had gone, then Beer nodded at Rylan, "You speak."

Dan Younge said, "I was just telling Wellman that people hate change. This is one that really upsets me. Are sergeants running the Army now?"

Beer said: "There are those who say they always did. Sergeant Rylan's been on the frontier ten years and more, I've been here two. We don't have a big enough command left to stand on formality. He's taking over till we fight our way out of Rock Spring."

Rylan said: "You stayed and fought with the boys today, and you got a brain, Mr. Younge. I've made up a plan. It listens good to the lieutenant, I want to hear what you think of it. After today, there's no use swapping words with the Shoshone; they wouldn't listen, right?"

Dan Younge said, "Right. But before you go on, I want to say that listening to you doesn't commit me to anything. I'm a gambler, not a crusader."

Beer said: "A crusader, Rylan, is a man who fights for a holy cause. Until you read history. Then you find out that they very often came home rich."

Dan Younge said: "What do you want of me?"

"To go on the malapie party. To help me raise a posse. Younge, a straight question. What about your sheriff?"

"I don't know him too well. Sheriffs and gamblers don't mix."

"I thought you must be his best friend. You were the only man with him out on the prairie."

Remembering Phyllis Sydnor and his reasons for riding out with Romayne, Dan Younge almost grinned. And then an idea came to him, an idea that would serve a great many purposes.

He said, "Oh, lieutenant, Romayne's another man like all of us. But I just thought of something. Sydnor, Charley Sydnor, carries great weight in this town. And he won't like the idea of able-bodied men going away, leaving him and his property unprotected."

"I know," Beer said.

Dan Younge said: "You'd better get him on your side—and I can tell you how."

Beer said: "You listening to this, Rylan?"

"This isn't for the sergeant. This you have to do yourself. Mrs. Sydnor," Dan Younge said from behind his best poker face, "is the real boss of that family." And forgive me for lying, Dear Lord. "Sydnor does anything she tells him to. And Mrs. Sydnor—I'm being delicate—would relish the attentions of a handsome young officer."

Beer looked startled, angry, perhaps even a little intrigued.

"For Rock Spring, for your country, for West Point," Dan Younge said, "You ought to see that she gets that attention. It shouldn't be too unpleasant."

Beer was frowning.

Rylan said: "I've seen her. A good lookin' lady."

Beer slapped the table. "The question is, if we decided to go into the malapie, are you coming with us?"

Dan Younge said carelessly. "Oh, sure. *If* you decide to go. I notice you're calling it malapie now, instead of malpais."

"Some of these local words are very interesting," Beer said, and got up to go.

Dan Younge watched them out the door. The Great Chance was staying active later than usual: there was quite a crowd at the bar. He could pull down his lamp, light it and get up a game. He might make quite a bit of money.

It had been a long day. He got his hat, strolled past the bar, and out into the street. There was a light in Sydnor's store. He remembered a player saying that the Sydnors had moved down there for safety, but he hadn't said safety from what.

Smiling his sardonic smile at the empty, starlit street, Dan Younge started his pre-bed stroll. He went up canyon, passed the Sydnor's house and then stopped. A lamp was lit in the kitchen, but the Sydnors were downtown…

He waited. After awhile the lamp was blown out, and then the backdoor opened.

There was no moon, but Sydnor's bulk was unmistakable. Another person, a man, followed him. Against the white of the house, whiskers bulked up the man's face—the miner Sergeant Rylan had wounded and captured.

The two men moved up the road towards the big rock, and Dan Younge followed.

He followed as Sydnor and his man skirted the Army camp, and then he got behind a little clump of young alders and just watched. Sydnor led the smaller man almost to the big rock. They disappeared there, and then after a while Sydnor came back, alone.

There was no noise of a sentry challenging. The miner had gone into a cave of some sort and Sydnor had helped him…

When Charley Sydnor had enough lead, Dan Younge followed him back down into town. The gambler was pleasantly tired now, his lungs full of fresh tobacco smoke. He was asleep before the clothes on his hotel chair were cold.

XIX

If groceries were getting more expensive in Rock Spring, the price of horses was going down. Dan Younge found this out the next morning when he started looking for a replacement for the mount that the miners had run off.

Animals that would have fetched two and three hundred dollars a week before were now offered freely for fifty, for twenty-five by men who did not see how they were going to feed them. Grazing was cut off, hay was running low.

He told a couple of men he'd maybe see them later, and went around to Sydnor. The merchant was in his store. He had buckled a gun around his girth and was supervising his wife and Ellen Lea as they waited on the customers. Business was brisk.

Dan Younge said: "I used your horse yesterday, and he's a good one. Do you want to sell him?"

Sell was a word that Charley Sydnor would always hear. He said, "He traces back to Justin Morgan on both sides. There isn't any better blood."

"That's why I want to buy him."

"How much was you thinking of paying?"

Phyllis Sydnor left the counter and came over. She spoke to her husband, but she stood so that her full skirt would conceal her hand, and she caught Dan Younge's fingers and squeezed them. She said, "Charles, Mr. Willows is asking for credit. He says the new prices have washed out all his cash reserve." Charley Sydnor said, "Willows has all his money tied up in freighting teams. Might be dead before this is over. Tell him to wait."

"Yes, Charles." She gave Dan's fingers a final caressing and was gone.

Dan Younge hoped the red in his face didn't show too much. "I need a horse," he said, and thought that he meant it now more than before. "And I'd like your Morgan. But there's many a good one going begging on the market. Say—sixty dollars."

Charley Sydnor's voice was gloomy as a hound dog's. "Coulda gotten three-fifty, maybe four hundred last week," he said. "He goes good in a harness, under saddle, he does it all."

"A good Morgan will," Dan Younge said. "Sixty dollars."

"Done," Charley Sydnor said. "I'll make you out a bill of sale." He stamped over to the standup desk, opened it, and rummaged for a paper.

Dan Younge took out his wallet, counted out bills; he'd drawn on the last two nights from Wellman to go buy his horse. If Rylan's plan works, he thought, I'll be out of here tomorrow, maybe…

"Good morning, Mr. Younge."

Dan bowed. "Mrs. Lea, you are looking well."

She was eyeing him with a certain sharpness he hadn't seen in her before. Either she'd noticed the lady's little handplay, or maybe Phyllis was being too open in the way she watched him. He looked over and decided that was it; she didn't like him talking to Ellen Lea. Oh, man, let me out of this jackpot.

Ellen Lea said softly: "You haven't changed your mind about working here?"

"Shotgun guard on a grocery store? No, I haven't changed my mind."

"Too bad," Ellen Lea said. "You'd have been someone to talk to." At once, as though she'd said too much, she was gone back to the counter, looking after the customers.

The horse was in a box stall. He went in with him, began running his hands over the Morgan's legs looking for flaws. This is the wrong way to go about it, he thought. Fault the horse first and buy him later is the way to end up rich.

A faint odor of cologne cut through the rich warm scent of the stable. He looked up. Phyllis Sydnor was leaning on the edge of the boxstall. "Dan," she said.

"Phyllis, you're crazy to come here."

"Nobody's interested in the stable. Nobody thinks they're going anyplace."

"But, Sydnor…"

"Shurtz sent over his boy for some groceries. Sydnor told me to go along and collect," she held up a hand full of money. "Charles isn't trusting anybody—unless they sign the pledge."

He felt stupid as he asked, "The pledge?"

"Some of the men are signing up not to go out on any posses, to stay and protect the store. Then he gives them credit. I'm sick of credit and cash and groceries and posses. Oh, Danny!"

He hated being called Danny. But she was opening the latch, coming into the boxstall. He said: "Careful, you don't want to get kicked."

"Oh, Ranger's a kitten, a little woolly lamb."

She almost leaned on the horse's haunch as she came towards Dan Younge, pressed herself into his arms. He was sweating from fear, but hardly from fear of Charley Sydnor. The storekeeper was no threat. Kill him now, and no man in town would serve on a hanging jury. Sydnor's profit-making use of the siege had taken care of that.

But the local bravos had their code, and one of its strictest rules was the protection (from everything but overwork) of the women. If he was caught compromising Phyllis Sydnor, he would have to marry her, and he had not bought a horse in order to settle down in Rock Spring with the lady.

On the other hand, a man refusing proffered feminine charms is an idiotic spectacle, and he has his own body to fight. Dan Younge's hands, all of Dan Younge, were trying to go towards the lady. Only his mind went the other way.

So, while he found himself putting his arms around her, he was looking desperately for someone to interrupt him.

She said, "Where can we meet tonight? I can make an excuse to Charles, get out of the store… Now that we've moved down there, I never get to see you anymore."

Her lips were against his chin. He ducked his head down

and kissed her, and she was cooperating enough to drive most of his worries out of his mind. But when the kiss was over, they crowded right back in on him, and some inner Dan Younge sneered at him. He wasn't man enough to pay for what he wanted.

He said: "I'm afraid we'll have to wait till the siege is lifted, and you're back in your own house, lady."

She moved away from him, both physically and sympathetically. "Maybe it's a good idea. I'm down at the store now. You were attentive enough to that Ellen Lea!"

"Ah, lady, I have to have an excuse to come into the store," Dan Younge said. "I can't buy something every time I want to see you."

Oh, break it up, the inner Dan Younge said. Face up to her. Tell her off!

But she was falling for it. "You're clever, lover." She moved in towards him again. She was, as he liked his ladies to be, a restrained user of perfume. The scent came up to him only when she was close, and warm and…

For God's sake, Younge, get hold of yourself.

He was saved by boots stamping down the runway of the stable. It was one of the soldiers. "Lieutenant wants to see you."

He placed the man as one who had gaily lost a month's pay in poker last night.

"Me, Haley? Or Mrs. Sydnor?"

Haley said: "You, mister," and turned away again.

Phyllis Sydnor said: "That was a curious question. Why should Mr. Beer want to see me?"

Dan Younge sighed. "Haven't you noticed him looking at you? No, you wouldn't. He's a shy young man; he's mostly sighed after you when your back was turned. I'm afraid you've broken another heart there, lady."

Phyllis Sydnor said: "Jealous, lover?"

"Not so long as you don't look back at him. I've got to go, lady. I'll see you in the store. I'll think of something to buy."

"Or come courting Ellen Lea," she said. "That looks natural enough."

Haley was waiting outside. He gave Dan Younge an amused grin and said: "I wouldn't mind a deal or two of that myself. The officer's in the hotel, him and Sarge Rylan. I'll walk across with you."

But he didn't need any guide to find Beer and Rylan. They, together with Jack Romayne, were the center of a knot of arguing men.

Dan Younge pushed his way into the center himself.

Beer said, "Glad you're here, Younge, we seem to have run into a squabble."

A voice said: "We don't need no gambler to tell us what's good for our town!"

Rylan's heavy voice answered before the lieutenant could. "Only one man in this town stood with the lieutenant and his boys yesterday. Only one was out with the sheriff when we first ran into your trouble here. I'd listen to Mr. Younge, gambler or horse thief or whatever he was!"

"Why shouldn't you?" someone asked. He shoved forward and it was Patson, the blacksmith, not a loudmouth. "You've got nothing to lose if they raid the town while you're gone. We've wives and children, homes and businesses."

Dan Younge said: "You'll lose them if you wait. We're in a trap here. It's up to us to fight our way out."

Rylan said, "There's so many of the Indians that if they decide to raid the town, a few defenders more or less won't help you. I'm asking twenty men to go with me, and four of our boys. Mr. Younge makes one. How about nineteen more?"

A man said, "We're having our government taken away from us by a soldier and a gambler! We goin' to stand for that?"

Dan Younge said, "That sounds like Willows' voice. Any of you know he's being paid by Sydnor to keep the men here to defend Sydnor's store?"

Willows said: "That's a lie." He was back in the crowd when

he said it, but somebody shoved him forward. Other men part-
ed to give him passage, and he ended up right in front of Dan
Younge.

Dan Younge said, "Well, say it again."

Willows shrunk back into the crowd, and Rylan got a laugh
by saying, "That one wouldn't do to take along, anyway. Anybody comin'?"

Amazingly Big Red, the bartender at the Great Chance,
stepped up. "Here goes nothing."

Wellman's voice came clear from the crowd. "Who's running my place tonight?"

Red's voice was respectful. "The day barman says he'll stay
on. And you can sit in for Dan Younge."

Rylan said, "We're not going on any long journey. They tell
me we can be at the malapie in less than two hours. How long
d'ya think a fight can last?"

Patson said: "No man does my fighting for me," and joined
Dan and Red.

That did it. The quota of twenty was filled in a few minutes
and the men scattered to get their horses.

Dan Younge led Ranger out of the stall, stepped to his back,
and jogged down the boards and out into the sun-drenched
street. There was a canteen tied to the cantle. He untied it and
carried it up to his hotel room, got his rifle and shotgun and
filled the canteen. By the time he'd tied all this on the saddle,
and ridden across the street to the store, half the possemen were
there.

Sydnor stood in the door of the store. Three or four men
were ranged behind him. When Dan Younge saw that one of
them was Willows, he knew what they were there for. Jack Romayne was nowhere in sight.

Sydnor said, "Now, I'm a man who speaks his mind, and
I'm saying that this whole posse's just a dodge for men to get
out of their natural duty, which is to stand up and defend their
homes."

"An' Sydnor's grocery store," one of the posse said. Dan Younge turned his head. It was Brister who'd said that. Brister added, "Charley's getting rich off our misery; no wonder he don't want them miners licked."

Sydnor said, "That'll be enough of that!" He suddenly unholstered his gun. "This store's mine, and I'll stand and fight for it. It's more'n you runaways'll do."

"Show you," said Patson, and hoisted his compact bulk forward. He walked up to Sydnor, right up to the barrel of the pistol. Then his heavy forearm chopped, and the gun clattered to the boards. "Bullets're under the back counter, boys. Take what you need."

Dan Younge went in with the rest. He swore at himself a little, because he felt ashamed to be doing what he was doing. It was theft. Necessary, of course, but he had never stolen before.

Ellen Lea looked at him. He looked away, and was staring straight into Phyllis Sydnor's eyes. He smiled at her, finished filling his belt and his pockets and looked further.

Sergeant Rylan was breaking open a case of cooking chocolate, passing the pound slabs of hard stuff out to his men. "We may be there all night," the sergeant said. "This'll keep you alive but it won't taste so good you'll eat it all first thing."

Dan Younge went over and got a slab of the bitter chocolate. "If it's good enough for the soldiers, it's good enough for us. We all better take some."

They tramped out of the store, mounted, and rode for the prairie, taking the trail he and Jack Romayne had taken, avoiding the Indian camp.

But they didn't avoid it by enough, they could hear chanting and drumming coming from there. "Funeral party," Rylan said, sitting arched in his saddle beside Dan Younge. "They lost a man or two in the ruckus yesterday."

"We're not doing this any too soon," Dan Younge said.

Rylan said, "No," and they rode on.

XX

All over the West, there are places that they call malapie in English, malpais—badlands—in Spanish. They are all alike, except in size: rolling deposits of black volcanic rock, looking like soft tar, full of pits and crevasses and caves where softer stone than the dense basalt has long ago weathered away.

The malapie near Rock Spring was about two miles wide and three long. No trail went near it, because the basalt was hell on horses' hooves. The heavy black rock was a great catcher of heat, and even skirting it a quarter of a mile away gave a man a killing thirst.

There were grassy patches between the rolling waves of black, shallow cracks that had trapped blowing dirt and grass seeds and grown up into something. There were other cracks too deep to fill up, and Rock Spring mothers before the siege had frightened their children with tales of people who had wandered into the malapie and never been seen again.

Also, it was good rattlesnake country.

Dan Younge had seen the malapie from a distance, rising from the prairie like an empty ship on the Mississippi, but he'd never been in it, or very near it.

They had left town at a steady lope, but as they got closer to the malapie, they began to drop down to a trot and then a walk, despite Rylan, who kept saying: "Keep up the canter, boys."

There was something about the black rocks looming ahead of them, getting larger all the time, that chilled a man's soul, Dan Younge thought. He wondered how the miners had gotten in there. Probably there had been posses from the Colorado camps after them.

He'd worked in a lot of goldfields in his time, and they were rough places. A man had to be pretty bad to get run out, and the gang that had stormed Rock Spring behind White Hat had looked bad enough.

He had a shotgun under his knee and a rifle across his saddle and a beltgun strapped on. A man ought to feel safe enough with all that armament, he thought, but he didn't feel safe. Yesterday he'd been a hero when he stayed and fought it out against the Indians, but it was easy to do that.

Going towards a fight was a lot harder than staying in one. He couldn't remember when he'd ever done anything like this before. He turned to Rylan and said, "They pay you fellows much for this sort of work?"

"Naw, but we get a military funeral." He rolled in his saddle, and cocked a bloodshot eye in a way that made Dan Younge laugh. The sergeant was out of uniform except for his yellow-striped blue pants. But as he stood in his stirrups and yelled, "Pick up the trot, Yoooh!" it would have been hard to mistake his calling.

Dan Younge lifted his reins and stood in his stirrups. If any of the men behind them felt reluctant about hurrying towards the malapie, their horses were fighting to keep up with the leaders. A man would have had to hold back on his lines enough to show, and that no man would do.

Dan Younge, his weight on his insteps, his rifle in his hand, thought they were getting awful close, within rifle shot. But no shot came, and he began to wonder. The miners must have been pretty desperate to raid the town the way they did. When the raid failed, maybe they took off, were starved out.

It was a cheery thought. As the big Morgan cut down the distance, it was a thought to cling to.

There was lava rock under their hooves now. Dirt had blown over it, and a thin mat of grass turfed it, but the hoofbeats had a different sound, a sort of drumming that they had lacked on the sandy prairie.

Then one of Ranger's hooves rang on bare lava, and they were in the malapie. Rylan raised his hand and brought down the clenched fist in the signal to walk, and for a moment the possemen bunched up behind them.

"Spread out, there," Rylan bawled. "Don't bunch up." He muttered something under his breath about damned civilians, and raised his voice again. "Schwartz, Haley, Harrington." Three of his troopers, all in half-uniform, came up. The fourth soldier, a corporal named Petty, was right behind them.

Rylan said: "Each of you take five men, dismount, and work one of these side canyons, line of skirmishers. Petty, take what's left as horseholders. You'll know how to cover them. I'll scout ahead of you, Schwartz, an' Dan Younge'll be picket man for Harrington on the other wing."

"You do me too much honor," Dan Younge said.

They were dismounting. Rylan bumped against Dan Younge. "Harrington's a young one," he said. "He knows just enough to stay the right distance behind a picket. Go slow and careful, and everything'll be fine. I brought him because he's a marksman."

Dan Young turned and looked the crowd over. "Which one's Harrington?"

The soldier who raised his hand looked young enough not to shave yet, but surely they didn't take them in the Army till their beards sprouted. Dan said: "I'm riding with you, Harrington."

There was a wild excited look in the youngster's eyes for a moment. Then he nodded, and said: "Yeah, I heard the sarge." He pointed: "You, you, you and you. You're in my detachment. Two of you on either side of me, an' th' gambler out front."

Dan was at his saddle, choosing. A man couldn't carry a rifle and a shotgun both. He looked over the men who were going to follow him. Harriman had his Army carbine, a townsman named Nelson had a rifle, the rest of them just beltguns. Well, a carbine and a rifle would do for the long distance work; he took his shotgun. A man gathered Ranger's reins in his hand with some others, said, "All right, boy," in an idle voice, perhaps ashamed to be back holding horses while other men went up into the malapie.

Harrington was pointing his men into position. The rifleman went on one side, Harrington himself closed the file on the other; the pistoleers filled in the middle. Dan Younge said: "I'll want at least fifteen feet between me and the line of skirmishers, or whatever you call it. Don't crowd me, and don't hurry me."

Harrington nodded without saying anything or looking at Dan Younge. He was watching Rylan. Finally the sergeant waved his hand, and Harrington said, "All right. Move out, gambler."

Dan Younge swung his fifteen feet up the canyon and started moving, swinging his head from side to side, watching, his shotgun crossed in front of him, hand on the trigger guard. His thoughts were idle. He thought that Harrington had been hurt bad at a gaming table more than once to talk that way to a man he hardly knew. He thought his black clothes were an asset in this black lava flow, and thinking that, pulled his black hat a little farther down on his forehead.

He thought that those handsome white clouds forming someplace behind the other edge of the malapie might bring thunderstorms on, though there'd been no rain for weeks. He thought that the little patch of grass he passed as he swung around a bend in the lava-fissure was so green it must mean a spring there. Might be a worthwhile project to dig it out, let it flow down to that patch of soil there, instead of going back into the rock.

He thought he might have made a farmer if things had been different. But being a farmer meant swapping with your neighbors—tools, labor, horses, bulls and studs—and a gambler'd never be welcome among farmers.

Now, ranching was something different. Ranching was being on your own. It was gambling, and the odds were way against you. A man who had been a houseman for all these years could never deal himself into a game against the house.

He thought idly of the ladies he'd known. There'd never been an Ellen Lea amongst them. That'd be marking the cards.

His ladies had always planned on getting their fun out of him without giving up the luxuries of their husbands, and that made it a fair game. What had gone wrong with Phyllis Sydnor?

He didn't like these thoughts, and cast around for some more. This malapie sure looked like tar, but it was one of the hardest rocks going. Must have been awful hot when…

Then he stopped thinking. A man had moved up there in the rocks. Just a flash of plaid shirt and a gray hat, but movement, and no animal. Dan Younge waved back to Harrington, and dropped on his belly, moving forward, keeping his rifle snugged under his chest, his belt pulled around so his Colt wouldn't be under him.

He moved forward on his elbow and hips, his boots raised a little from the rocky ground. He didn't know it, but he didn't want the rough lava scuffing leather off his forty-five dollar black footwear; in fact he would have been shocked if he'd known that part of him was capable of thinking of a thing like that at a time like this.

Around a round black rock, like a huge toadstool. Down into a smooth crease into the lava, then up again, through a sloping alley covered with rubble that dug into his elbows.

Now. Now he ought to be able to see his man. There, where green moss had obscured the black of the malapie, there, and…

He saw the man, clearly, for a moment, a man in a faded shirt that had once been fiesta gay, in soiled fawn pants with patches on the knees, in a sweat-stained gray hat. He saw him clearly enough to see all these things, and was puzzled by what the man was doing; for the miner wore no gun and carried neither shotgun nor rifle. He was just bending down, picking up something, taking a bite at it…

Reluctant to shoot an unarmed man, Dan Younge held his fire, and lived to regret it forever. The stick of dynamite that the man had just crimped with his teeth flew over Dan Younge's head and landed square among the men of Harrington's little command.

Dan Younge, against his will, twisted back to look. Harrington, indeed, had had the fault Rylan had named. He had been too eager, he had not waited for Dan Younge to report. If he'd laid back where he'd been told to, he would have been out of range.

But he'd never take the lash of Rylan's tongue for his fault. He was gone, and his men were gone, blown into unrecognizable fragments of horror, and the rest of the blast spilt a small piece of malapie and sent it down over them for a tombstone.

This Dan Younge saw, and twisted back, and the miner in the plaid shirt was standing there, crimping down another cap to another stick. For a miracle he had not seen Dan Younge, and the oversight cost him his life.

Dan Younge shot him, and watching the dingy shirt turn bright and catch the sun as the buckshot hit home. Then the miner fell, and the cap must have been tight and ready, for the stick of dynamite blew up under him.

But he had been dead already.

XXI

Lava country is tricky country. Voices bounce off the smooth walls of the black rock; and one fissure looks precisely like the next. Stories are told of travelers who went into the malapie to explore, and died, lost, while a hundred yards away a companion or a wife called them back to safety.

Around Dan Younge now there was a confusion of voices, of noises of all kinds. Some more dynamite had gone off someplace, and someplace else Sergeant Rylan was shouting and other voices could be heard, too. But where they were or whose voices they were, he couldn't decide; and he couldn't make out what the sergeant was saying.

He decided to go ahead. Not knowing anything about the geography of the malapie, he had as good a chance of circling back by going forward as not; and the truth was, he didn't want to go through the little canyon where Harrington and his men had been blown up.

He was drenched with sweat, his eyes smarted from it. The black rocks caught and trapped the heat, saved it to punish intruders to their depths.

That is mighty fancy thinking, Dan Younge told himself, and wriggled on.

It was not purpose, just accident, that brought him around a bend in the lava, and square upon the miner he had shot.

The man was not as badly mangled as he'd expected. Some trick of dynamite had sent most of the powder stick's force sideways and down so that the body was lying in a hole, but from the back it had not been disintegrated the way Harrington and his men had been.

There was a box of dynamite and a box of caps near the dead man's hand. Dan Younge sat up on his heels and considered this. He had a mighty weapon in his hands; but he didn't know how to use it. He'd never shot off a stick in his life, never even been near anyone who was blasting. He was a gambler, not a miner.

It might well cost him his life. Explosions were going off from time to time in other parts of the malapie; men were screaming, men were shouting, and once he was pretty sure that he heard Rylan shouting for the horses.

There were gunshots, too, and some of these must be the possemen. But what could gunslingers do against dynamiters, especially when the dynamiters had better knowledge of the rocks? A good powderman on the side of the law could turn the battle, *if* he had the dynamite.

Dan Younge had the dynamite, but he didn't know how to use it.

For the first time, he felt absolute fear. Not just worry, but the almost certain knowledge that he was trapped in the malapie, that it would only be a matter of time before the miners hunted him down and blew him up.

His one chance was to get to other possemen, turn his powder over to them, and hope that one of them knew how to use it. He heaved the two boxes up, aware that the one thing he knew about dynamite was that caps and sticks should be kept apart.

There were labels tacked to the little boxes; one of the tacks stuck out and tore at his hand. He took out his pocketknife to pull the tack, and read the label.

The dynamite had been sent from a Chicago wholesaler to Charles Sydnor, Rock Spring.

A whole lot of things became clear at once. Sydnor getting the wounded miner into what Dan had thought was a cave, but which must have been a rock tunnel out of town; the activities around the store at night; Sydnor's furious attempts to keep the posse home. Charley Sydnor was a traitor in the simplest sense of the word, a renegade, a man who'd see his neighbors killed for his profit.

The fear that had filled Dan Younge was gone. An anger he didn't know he had owned took its place. He'd been a fool, an idiot who risked his life simply because his life didn't mean much to him. It did now. Life meant a chance to get back at Charley Sydnor.

The sardonic humor with which Dan Younge armored himself against the world was gone, and he didn't know how he'd shed it. He didn't stop to wonder why he wanted to kill Charley Sydnor; it didn't occur to him to think that it was none of his business. He just wanted to kill.

It was probably the first time in his life that a single passion had moved Dan Younge.

He clutched the two boxes to his belly and, bent over, started hurrying back along the way he had come. But the tricky canyons fooled him. In a few minutes he was back at the place where he'd found the dead man and the dynamite.

He straightened up, gasping, and a bullet clipped air near his head.

He bellied down again. The sound of the shot was echoing all around him, louder than the booms of the dynamite sticks still going off in the near distance. It was impossible for him to tell where the shot had come from, and now that he was down on the ground, it was apparently impossible for the gunman to see him.

He left his powder and his caps on the floor of the canyon, raised his shotgun breast high, and slowly stood.

He was lucky. He was facing the man, a man in a black shirt, standing on a chunk of malapie, holding a pistol. They both fired at the same time, and again the bullet went high, and apparently the shotgun could not carry that far, because the miner still stood, though Dan was sure his aim had been good.

He dropped the spattergun and snatched at his belt, and the miner fired and knicked cloth from Dan Younge's shoulder.

He couldn't be killed. He felt armored in his hatred for Charley Sydnor. He pulled trigger on the miner, once and then twice, and the second bullet hit the outlaw as he was already going down.

Dan Younge snatched up his boxes and charged forward, the shotgun under his arm. He scrambled over the slick rocks and got to the blackshirted body.

The miner had picked a good place for his stand. Dan Younge could see into a dozen of the crooked passages through the black rocks. He spotted Rylan, making a stand, spreading his men around to pin down the miners. A couple of the miners were visible too. Dan Younge fished shells from his pocket, reloaded the barrels of the shotgun, blasted at the nearest patches of miners' clothing.

Then he snatched up the boxes and plunged from rock to rock toward Rylan, exposing himself because he didn't dare get down in the cover and get lost.

Rylan was shouting: "Now! Bring up them horses, now!" His cavalry boom carried clear and commanding in the hot air. Dan Younge jumped another little canyon and Rylan stood up. Dan got both the small boxes under his left arm, tossed the shotgun to the sergeant, who caught it and hung on to it.

Then Dan Younge was there, and the horseholders were running up, the horses plunging and trying to tangle their lines. Rylan was bold, running to tap men, shouting, "You, and you and you—mount up an' ride." The sergeant got to Dan Younge's horse, swapped the shotgun for the rifle, and came trotting back, leading the horse. "You an' me'll fight rearguard." He raised his voice. "Everybody mount up! Put 'em at the gallop, an' keep it up."

A horseholder shoved reins in Rylan's hands. He looped the leather around his arm, and made him stand with his carbine, squeezing off a shot almost at once. Dan Younge stood by his side, half turned away. He saw a movement in the malapie and fired and knew he'd hit nothing, but the man he'd shot at did not appear to fire or heave dynamite after the possemen.

Horses drummed behind Dan Younge and Rylan, loud at

first, and then fainter, and Rylan said quietly, "We'll ride for it, now," and at once jumped into the saddle.

Dan Younge picked up his boxes again. Rylan was already on his way, but he wheeled his horse back and shoved one box between his belly and the phantom cantle of his McClellan saddle.

Dan Younge managed to scramble aboard his horse holding the other box and the rifle and his reins all anyway in his hands. He swung his heels and Ranger took off, fast. Dan bent low and when the bullets started following them, he and the sergeant were out of range.

"All right," Rylan called. "They're not followin'. No use killing two horses."

They pulled down to walk. "We led 'em in," Rylan said. "You and me. Reckon it was up to us to guard 'em out."

"We got away with it," Dan Younge said.

"We got away with nothin'," the sergeant said. His voice was bitter; there were lines along his thin-lipped mouth that had not been there before. "I lost two-thirds of my men! I ought to have my stripes ripped off! I ought to be stable police the rest of my enlistment!"

"I shot two of the miners," Dan Younge said. "Killed 'em."

"And I the same, and the other boys a half dozen more. But there's ten, twelve of the snakes left in those black rocks, an' the price we paid was too high."

"It wasn't necessary," Dan Younge said. "The whole thing wasn't needed."

Rylan turned in the saddle to stare. "And what are you trying to say? This some of your fancy gamblin' talk?"

"Nothing fancy about it. We could have stayed home, lynched one man, and made starve-outs of the miners." He gestured. "Read the label on that box."

Rylan looked down at his cantle. "Blasting caps! Man, an' me galloping with my old belly rubbing that!" He made to throw the box away.

"No, the other label. The address."

Rylan looked. His hand came up and pulled his horse to a dead halt. "Rock Spring! So the powder that blew those boys away was from their own storekeeper." He shook his head. "I've heard of that kind, but I never figured to get to spoil a bullet on one."

"A rope'll do," Dan Younge said. "This is no Army funeral."

"A rope it'll be," Rylan said. "And some satisfaction. But it'll be cold. It'll be cold comfort for those boys dead back there, and not enough of them to bury."

XXII

They overtook the posse after a while, sitting on the prairie, munching on the hard chocolate Rylan had looted from Sydnor's store. Seven men, the soldier Haley and six townsmen, and Haley and a townsman were wounded, their shirts torn to make rude bandages.

Rylan and Dan Younge swung down to join them. "Indians ahead," the stocky Patson said. "They've been ahead all the way. Flickering ahead, like lights in a swamp."

"Watching us," Dan Younge said. "Could be that they've figured out we're trying to deal truly with them, trying to get them the murderers of their people."

Rylan said gloomily: "I know Indians. One white man's much like another to them. Could be, all they know is the whites are fighting each other at last, and making it good weather for Indians." He stood up, wiping a smear of chocolate off his mouth with the back of his hand. "Might as well go to town. I lost three troopers. How many of the others were married men?"

"We were figuring," Patson said. "All but Big Red, the barkeep."

"Let's go to town," Rylan said. "It'll be no fun there."

They mounted again and moved out, Dan Younge and Rylan and the wounded Trooper Haley riding together, three men not of the town, though they had fought Rock Spring's battle. Twice Rylan pointed, and Dan Younge saw the broomtail of an Indian pony disappear down a draw.

Finally the sergeant spoke. "Show Haley the label, Younge."

Dan Younge handed the box over for Haley to hold in his one usable hand. "I wondered why you didn't show it back at the rest," he said. "But I followed your lead."

"I don't know why anyone would follow me, after what I led

us into today," Rylan said. His gloom was heavy on him. "But I'm somewhat cooled now. No use hangin' your Mr. Sydnor till we've tolled them renegades into his store. They used a lot of dynamite today. Could be the night'll see them trying to buy more."

"Yes, but…" Dan Younge swallowed. "Knowing what we're knowing, are we going to look at Sydnor and not spit?"

"My observation has been, you're no Sydnor kisser at the best of times," Rylan said. "For all your Mr. Sydnor's money."

Haley suddenly chuckled. "Depends on which Sydnor you mean, Sarge."

Dan Younge remembered Trooper Haley coming into the livery stable, interrupting the little scene of love or passion or intrigue or whatever it was in Ranger's stall. It seemed a long time ago and a long ways away, and now, his body exhausted by the battle, his mind by the constant push of hunting out the miners without himself being hunted, he couldn't remember why he'd pursued Phyllis Sydnor.

He said: "Last I saw, your lieutenant was thinking along those lines."

"She's too good for an officer," Haley said. "You seen her, Sarge?"

Rylan grunted. "I'm thinkin' of war and the ways of war," he said. "Tonight we'll spread out around Sydnor's store, block the alley both ways, put one man on the street. I'd like to be one ways up the alley, for all I haven't slept since General Grant was a corporal. Haley, you're on sick call."

"I'll take the other end," Dan Younge said. "Maybe Beer would do for the street."

"Fair enough," said Rylan, and they rode on.

Dark was coming now, and distant on the prairie, lights began to flicker. Rylan sighed, deep from his chest, and Dan Younge said: "What is it, Sarge?"

"Why, Indian fires," Rylan said. "Like we mighta known. They've had their pow-wow, an' some have said we're acting with good hearts, trying to lay the murderers low. And others have said that the only good white man's a dead white man, which is the way young Haley here thinks of officers, and maybe sergeants, too."

Haley chuckled, and then stopped.

Dan Younge said: "Is that good? It means we have a divided enemy."

Sergeant Rylan was heavy in his voice, a drillmaster talking to recruits. "In the time when I first drew Western duty," he said, "there was a prosperity on the land, and almost every lieutenant carried a colonel's brevet in his pocket, from the war. So we who rode the Indian land were honored with the leadership of many a European officer—mercenaries, though they preferred the title of professionals. Italians, Frenchmen, plenty of Germans, some Irish, and them no better than the others. The brevet colonel-lieutenants, you see, preferred duty at Fort Myers and Governor's Island. 'Twas then I heard the silly talk you have been talking, Dan Younge. Divide the Indians and beat them. Maybe it's good when you're fighting Russians, or maybe so the kind of Indians that Englishmen fight, but this kind, now, you divide them, and you have a hundred little bands, each of which'll kill a couple of white men, take the scalps and ride off."

Dan Younge said: "I see."

"From now on, there'll be no Rock Spring Reservations Shoshone. But the Snakes and the Cheyennes, the Wasatch Utes and a dozen other tribes'll each have a few more people in it. Can you tell one Indian from another, if he changes his name and his pony, his head-band and his way of talking?"

Dan Younge said: "No."

"So let us each write his name down the way he wants it on the graveboard, in case there's any left to bury scalpless bodies. But I'm taking some of those murdering miners with me, if I'm lucky. We'll stake out tonight."

Haley said: "He's a gloomy one, the sarge. And talkative."

But Haley wasn't laughing and neither was Rylan or Dan Younge. They rode on to town with their handful of posse-men behind them.

Rock Spring was armed and patrolled. A sentry challenged them a hundred yards out of the town, another where the board sidewalks started. The second one was a soldier; he said, "Lieutenant's declared martial law, Sarge."

Rylan said: "Ay," and rode on. At the livery stable he said: "Later, then, Dan," and went up the street towards the military camp, his wounded trooper still beside him.

The possemen were scattering to their homes. The streets were quiet, the Great Chance closed. Martial Law. Dan Younge unsaddled and rubbed Ranger down well, baited the horse's manger and hayrack, and then took off his shirt and scrubbed in the livery stable horse trough.

He was fiercely dirty; he hadn't realized it before. He wanted a bath, hot and all over, but it wasn't worth while waking the barber who owned all of Rock Spring's public bathtubs.

Then he remembered. The barber was dead. His name had been Codlin, and he was out in the malapie someplace, what was left of him. His widow owned the bathtubs and the barber chair and the razors and shaving mugs now.

Dan Younge slapped himself dry and pulled his filthy shirt on again. He went on down the runway, and out onto the Main Street. Quiet. The closing of the saloon, the declaring of martial law, had kept the people in their houses; it seemed nobody knew the posse was back yet. In the morning, women would come out with their garbage, with their washing, and see that a neighbor's husband was home, would ask about her own man—and then there would be wailing, there would be curses called down on the heads of the men who had led the townsmen out into the malapie.

Until the Indians struck, until the miners struck, and then there'd be nothing—a big rock with water gushing out from under it, some rock-lined holes where foundations had been, some half burnt timbers.

There were lights in the sheriff's office, in the hotel, in Sydnor's store. Dan Younge stood looking. A woman's figure hitched across Sydnor's lamplight, but he couldn't make out whether it was Ellen Lea or Phyllis Sydnor.

He turned towards the hotel. They'd give him food there, and he could take a can of hot water up to his room and maybe get a good washdown before Rylan sent for him.

But, in turning, his eyes raked the sheriff's office. The broken glass had been replaced with oat sacking, and light showed through in a hundred pinholes. They outlined another woman— or the sheriff had grown a bosom and hips.

He went that way, his heels loud on the boardwalk, then his knuckles loud on the door. Jack Romayne called for him to come in, and he opened the door.

Romayne was at his desk, fiddling with some papers that would, now, never get filed. Ellen Lea was moving around the place with a peacock feather duster, tidying up.

Coming on him fresh from the hell of malapie and prairie heat, from the dour sight of the Indian fires, it almost made Dan Younge laugh, this calm sight of a woman dusting and a man filling out forms. He said: "We're back, sheriff."

Romayne looked up, startled. "I didn't hear you come into town."

"Not enough of us to raise a dust," Dan Younge said.

Jack Romayne didn't get it. He even smiled, and maybe that would be the last smile in the short history of Rock Spring. "You did a quick job," he said. "I've been sitting here thinking I should have gone with you, but you didn't need me."

"That's right," Dan Younge said. He'd always been a man of careful diction, but he could hear a drawl creeping into his voice now. "That's right. One more man blown to hell wouldn't have helped a bit."

Ellen Lea dropped the feather duster. Jack Romayne pushed his chair away from his desk. Romayne said: "Blown up?" His voice cracked and he squeaked.

"Dynamite," Dan Younge said. "That malapie's like a fort. They just hid behind the boulders and heaved sticks of powder at us. Eight of us came back."

Jack Romayne said: "I've got to see Sydnor." He stumbled from behind the desk and half skidded across the office, and was gone. The oatsack window fluttered for a minute and was still.

Ellen Lea said, "That seems to be that."

Dan Younge said, "I'm sorry," though he wasn't quite sure what he was sorry for. Love's young dream—and Ellen Lea wasn't that young—destroyed didn't seem too important in a town that was about to be burnt down, to a girl whose scalp would probably ride on an Indian's waist tomorrow or the next day.

That hair—he'd never noticed before—seemed to be in two braids wrapped around Ellen Lea's head. He wondered what it would look like down, and then wondered if he was thinking of passion—or scalping.

Stop thinking, Dan. He said: "A lot to do tonight. I'm going to wash up and eat at the hotel. Would you eat with me?"

Ellen Lea nodded and said: "I'll meet you in the dining room in a quarter of an hour." He turned away and would have left, but she spoke again. "I'm sorry," she said. "Women are awful fools. It doesn't make much difference now that I was in love with a coward and a braggart, does it?"

The lobby of the hotel was filling up. Dan Younge had never been in a town under martial law before, but he supposed that Beer's orders had been against men ganging up on the street. Since the Great Chance was closed, the hotel lobby was the only place where fearful men could try to borrow courage from each other.

Shurtz was near the desk. Dan Younge went over and said, "I asked Mrs. Lea to supper with me. Can you feed us?"

"Chipped beef, creamed. Some canned vegetables an' fried

potatoes. We're feeding everybody the same."

"It'll do fine. She'll be here any minute."

Shurtz nodded, but he didn't turn away. Finally he said: "Mr. Younge…"

Dan said nothing. He had a pretty good idea of what was coming.

"If you could settle your bill tonight. I mean, with the Army taking over…"

Dan Younge didn't see what the Army had to do with it. But this was pretty good evidence that the news of the posse's defeat and the Indians' breakout was through the town. If Shurtz was going to be killed, he'd want to die with as much money in his pocket as possible; or maybe the possession of money was a comfort to him, a charm against death.

Dan started to reach for his pocket, and thought better of it. He suppressed a smile, and stepped to the desk, took a sheet of hotel letterpaper, and wrote on it: "Mr. Wellman, please pay Mr. Shurtz my hotel bill out of what I have coming to me," and signed it, handed it over. "This'll more than cover it."

Shurtz looked unhappy, but there wasn't anything he could do about it.

Dan Younge went out on the porch. After awhile Ellen Lea came up and he rose to offer her an arm and lead her into the dining room.

Seated, he said, "Here goes your reputation, eating with a gambler."

"That hardly matters," Ellen Lea said, in her direct way. "I don't say that because it's now, the end of Rock Spring. But because people who'd look down on me for going with a gambler aren't people whose opinions ever mattered. Not ever."

The waitress was putting unappetizing looking plates of food in front of them. Dan Younge let her get away before he said, "Never?"

Ellen Lea said, "Not since I was a silly goose aged thirteen."

Dan Younge said: "I got an idea you're maybe a little smarter than I am. I think maybe I've been a little too ready to imagine people looking at me cross-eyed because of what I am."

Ellen Lea said: "I was about to say you seemed different from most gamblers, but it just occurred to me you're about the only one I ever knew."

They ate then, heartily, considering the poor quality of the food. Ellen Lea said: "The cook ran out of town some time this afternoon, while you were over at the malapie. Almost a hundred people have slipped out Jack Romayne says."

Dan Younge looked up quickly, to see if she'd mentioned the sheriff by mistake, if she was sorry for it. But she was forking potatoes into her mouth. She ate with an unladylike gusto that was, somehow, good to see. A man would keep his appetite eating with a girl like that year after year.

Aware of the trend of his thoughts, he spoke, "With Shoshone all over the prairie, and a good part of them hostile, you can say goodbye to anybody out there alone. People should have stayed in town."

"Dan, you weren't surprised when Jack Romayne fell apart before."

Dan Younge shrugged.

Ellen said: "I guess he did it before. Maybe when you and he went out after the murderers, the first time. He asked me to marry him. Maybe I would have, I'm lonely enough, goodness knows, and he's fun to talk to. I guess you'd say that wasn't much reason to get married, though."

Dan Younge said nothing for a moment. Then he said: "Even if the people who slipped out of town fell in with the part of the Indians who don't want a war, it won't do them any good. The friendly Shoshone won't kill them, but they won't help them or stop the other Indians from killing them."

"I guess I got put in my place," Ellen Lea said. "I'm a woman who says what's on my mind. I hoped you'd be the same sort of man."

Dan Younge got up, put a two-bit piece under the edge of his plate—the waitress might as well die happy—and said, "Thanks for eating with me. I like to talk my mind out, too, and what I gotta say is this. If we weren't all going to be killed tonight or maybe tomorrow, I'd sure like a chance at running that well rig you own. But that's an easy thing to say when time's run out, and who'd believe me?"

"Why, I would," Ellen Lea said. She stood up, too. "And if Mr. Beer's men weren't poking bulls' eye lamps into every dark corner of town, I would be pleased to let you kiss me." And she walked away, leaving Dan Younge gaping after her.

A moment later he was chuckling. She had taken that hand, and she had taken it on a bluff. You might say she'd beaten a full house with two pairs. It was something that had seldom been done to him.

XXIII

Sergeant Rylan was back in uniform; incredibly neat and well-brushed and shaved after his day in the malapie. Dan Younge sat down next to him on the porch and passed over one of two cigars he'd bought in the lobby.

The sergeant bit off the end of the cigar, spat it into the street, accepted a light. He was no longer the sorrowing, beaten commander of the afternoon. The past was past, and he was simply a soldier resting up for whatever trouble lay ahead.

Someone was coming down the boardwalk fast. From the sound of the heeltaps, it was a woman.

Rylan said: "Oh, lord. Another wife to tell me I killed her husband."

Dan Younge said: "Have much of that?"

"Two. One of them didn't know what she was sayin'. Mrs. Patson went out of her way to tell me it wasn't my fault, which helped some, not enough…"

The woman burst up on the porch. Two of the men on patrol were right behind her. Rylan waved them away; she was Ellen Lea. The sergeant started to get up. She said: "No, I've something I want to tell you both."

Then she stopped and looked around. Dan Younge was on his feet, his hand stretched out towards her, but she spoke to the sergeant. "Jack Romayne just came to me. Charley Sydnor's getting out of town, tonight, early tomorrow morning, while it's still dark. He told Jack about it. Jack's going along, as a bodyguard. There's a secret way out, your sentries don't know about it."

Rylan looked up at Dan Younge, and then they slowly nodded.

Dan Younge said: "He's the same to the end. He figured like

we did; there'll be a big sale made around midnight. Then he'll go away with his friends… Ellen, Jack wanted you to go with him?"

"I couldn't leave Rock Spring just now," Ellen Lea said. "A man just offered to take over my well rig and run it for me. I couldn't leave that."

Rylan said: "Stay in the hotel, and away from windows. That Romayne ain't much, but he might work himself up to shooting a woman from a dark street." Then, remembering, perhaps, that Rock Spring had named Ellen Lea Jack Romayne's girl, he said, quickly, "A man under fear of death should not be judged."

Dan Younge moved his thumb a little and Ellen Lea saw the gesture; she went on into the hotel lobby. Dan turned to Rylan, "You'll want Lieutenant Beer to know about this. It's my thought that I should be the one to tell him."

Rylan said: "I wish we knew where Sydnor's way out of town was."

"I know," Dan Younge said. "I've known quite awhile."

"You could have…" Rylan said.

Dan Younge cut him off. "It wasn't any of my business," he said. "I'll see Beer." He went off the porch, fast, passed the patrols without being challenged, then was at Sydnor's back door. He couldn't remember that he had ever gone through the front door of this house. Well, he'd be consistent on this, his last visit.

He opened the door and went in. There was no light showing anyplace. He stood at the foot of the backstairs and called: "Lieutenant! Lieutenant Beer!"

There was some noise from upstairs. Dan Younge felt his old sardonic grin coming over his face, felt his old, sour joy in telling the world to go to hell.

Upstairs a door opened, a match was struck, and the stench of sulphur drifted down to Dan. Then a lamp wick caught, and there was the clink of glass as the chimney was put on the lamp.

Looking up, Dan could see Beer standing at the head of the

stairs, holding the lamp up. The lieutenant was in uniform and campaign hat, the broad black brim shaded his face so that it was hard to see if that face was red. He called, "Who's there?"

"Rylan sent me, lieutenant. Message for you."

The lamp would not shine down the stairs, show Beer who was talking. He started down, carrying the light. When he came even with Dan Younge, he missed his lamp again, and this time there was no doubt about it. He was blushing.

Dan Younge said, "You've been dealing with the enemy, Beer?"

Beer said: "Talk sense."

"Sydnor, Jack Romayne, maybe some more, plan to make a break out of town to the malapie, go away with the miners. I imagine they plan on taking the lady with them." He gestured upstairs, keeping his face solemn.

Beer frowned. "If they go out of town the Indians will kill them."

"Not them. It's a short run to the malapie, and they'll be going with the miners."

Beer said a curious thing. He said: "Damn a man who'd take a woman to an outlaw camp. Sydnor ought to have more sense, more decency."

Dan Younge chuckled. "Two objections. One, I don't know your definition of a lady, but I imagine it doesn't include the kind upstairs. Two, it's run for the malapie or get killed, and Sydnor's got money tied up in his Phyllis. He wouldn't want to leave her for the Shoshone."

Beer swore. "I'd better get downtown."

"Yep," Dan Younge was grinning now. "You better bring the lady, too."

But Beer stood a moment more, then, when he saw that Dan Younge was making no move to go ahead of him, he shrugged his blue shoulders and went upstairs again, leaving Dan Younge in the dark.

A murmur of voices came back down, and then the light reappeared, and Beer was giving Phyllis Sydnor an arm down the stairs. She had on a buff serge riding outfit, long skirt over the boots, and she had never looked more beautiful.

She looked at Dan and bowed and said, "Good evening, Mr. Younge," and it was all over. This was one town he could stay in, and not run away from a lady.

It was too bad that it was a town that was about to blow itself off the earth.

XXIV

They walked downtown in silence, the three of them. They passed no one but the patrols. Rock Spring had gone to bed, or had congregated in the hotel.

Rylan stood up when his officer came on the hotel porch. "All quiet, sir. I broke the town up. Women are in the hotel, men I got over in the livery stable and the corral. Haley's in charge of keeping them there, and patrols are out."

Beer nodded. "How's Haley's wound?"

"He can handle a pistol all right. The ladies are in the hotel, Mrs. Sydnor. If you'll go into the lobby."

She said: "My husband's waiting for me over in his store. It's close by, we'll…"

Beer turned to Rylan. "Got a couple of men on hand, sergeant?"

"Well, I made militia out of a few townsmen—" It was obvious that Rylan was enjoying this.

Beer turned back to the lady. "I'd hate to have to use force." Phyllis Sydnor came apart then. She grabbed at Beer's shirt. "You've got to let me go, go back to the store!" She shook him, and her voice rose to a scream. "My husband just let me go home to put on these clothes, he's waiting, I have to go…"

People, mostly women, were crowding out of the lobby, staring curiously, as Phyllis Sydnor shook Beer. "I tell you, I have to go back, got to, gotta…"

Beer made a motion with his hand. Rylan, no longer grinning, reached out for the lady's shoulders. She evaded him and grabbed Dan this time. "Dan, make him, make him let me go back, lemme, lemme…"

Dan twisted loose, and Rylan grabbed her. He thrust her towards the lobby door. "Miz' Lea, some of you women, get her in there, keep her. She's not to get out."

Phyllis Sydnor screamed, piercingly. Her hair was coming down over her eyes, a button had burst open among the lace on her bosom, the heavy serge riding skirt had swiveled around and hung draggle-tailed from her hips. But her eyes were dry. "You got to, got to, lemme go—"

Ellen Lea had her now. The girl, slimmer than Phyllis Sydnor, was showing remarkable strength. She twisted Phyllis' arm behind her and clapped the other hand over the older woman's mouth. "She'll stay here if I have to tie her," Ellen Lea said, panting. Her blouse had pulled away from one shoulder, disclosing a series of silk straps. But suddenly she grinned at Dan Younge, and then, more briefly, at Beer. "Don't worry," she said. "She'll stay here—and quiet—if I have to put her in Mr. Shurtz's icebox."

Beer was telling the wide-eyed women in the doorway that Mrs. Sydnor was under arrest, that he'd explain it later.

Rylan had gone back to the command desk. The women had drifted back into the lobby, craning their necks up the hotel staircase. No doubt Ellen Lea had taken the lady up there and was now tying her to a bed.

Dan Younge said, "Beer, let's put a little strategy and tactics to this mess."

They pulled up porch chairs on either side of Rylan's. Dan said, "With your permission, gentlemen, I'll review the situation."

Rylan's expression was one of complete amazement.

Beer said, "Sergeant, our gambling friend's got a resurgence of hope."

"It's a long word for going daft," Rylan said. "Hope's not a thing I'd look around for just now. Not in Rock Spring."

Dan Younge said: "It's nothing to you and me, sarge. Just our lives. But to Mr. Beer, now, it's a chance to take a step towards that generalship he aims for."

"For a noble defense of the town of Rock Spring, Second

Lieutenant James V. Beer is hereby posthumously brevetted First Lieutenant, and his grave shall be marked accordingly."

"My gawd," Rylan said, "I've soldiered with this officer for a year and over, an' he finally made a joke."

Dan Younge said intently, "We're on the bottom. We've got no place to go but up, to victory, to use a fancy word. We can be reasonably certain of one thing: the miners are going to come into town, probably tonight, certainly within a night or two."

"Make it tonight," Rylan said. "That's my department."

Beer said, "I can take two troopers and wipe them out as they come out of the tunnel under the rock, the cave, whatever it is. Incidentally, you'd better show it to me."

"Yes," Dan Younge said. "Now, leave that enemy alone for the minute; take the next one."

"The Indians?" That was Rylan. His voice was heavy again. "Too many and too scattered for the men over in the livery stable, supposing they'd fight."

Dan Younge said: "The second enemy is Sydnor. And his force, which, so far as we know, consists of Jack Romayne, and a sad-eyed weeper named Willows."

Beer said: "We can tie them up with one length of clothesline. And that leaves the Indians."

Dan Younge said at once, "We don't bother Sydnor and Romayne, we don't bother the miners. We use them as bait to draw the Shoshone off."

Lieutenant Beer's reaction was simple. He asked one word, "How?"

Dan Younge stared out at the deserted street. "They tell me Indians talk with those drums we're hearing."

Rylan said, "That's right. They can pass quite a message along."

"So all I have to do is get to one Indian camp—anyone with a drummer—and they'll be able to send for that squaw man, what's his name, Nate Allen?"

Suddenly Rylan said, "Someone's coming out of Sydnor's

store." His voice snapped. "You, Strayne! Parley here! Cover it." A trooper materialized out of the night, and brought his carbine up across his chest and stood waiting. "It's Sydnor," Rylan said. "I'll wash the other up fast for you, Dan. I can give you the Indian's sign for peace, the way to hold your hand, hold your horse's bridle. I can give you the Ute word for the same thing, to shout, and I hear the Shoshone talk much the same as the Ute. I can give you no hope that it'll work, and I'm a sorry kind of Indian expert at best."

Sydnor was not ten feet away now. Beer said sharply, "I'll do the talking, and I don't expect to be interrupted."

Charley Sydnor blustered up to Rylan's desk, and slapped it hard with his beefy hand. "My wife went up-canyon to our house an hour and more ago. I want her back. Your damned tin soldiers won't let me go!"

Lieutenant Beer said, "Your wife is in the hotel. She'll stay there."

Sydnor said: "I want her back. I…"

Beer made an almost imperceptible gesture, and the guard dropped his carbine so that it pointed straight at Charley Sydnor. The storekeeper slapped out at the barrel of the gun. Strayne stepped back, and Sergeant Rylan said: "Ready! Aim…"

Sydnor's face was purple in the light that beamed from the hotel. He took a couple of deep breaths, then turned and pounced across the dusty street to his store.

Beer said softly, "What do you make of that?"

Dan Younge said, "There's a desperate man. I think he thinks the miners won't take him along if he hasn't women, or a woman, to offer them. I expected him to demand Ellen Lea, too, and if he had, I would have…"

Beer said, "And Sergeant Rylan would have broken your wrist. We need him alive and in his store. For the ambush of the miners."

Dan Younge said, "All right. I leave now, and then you let Sydnor and the miners go. Meanwhile, I'll have gotten to the

Indians, told them the men they want are coming out of town. It may hold them."

Beer said: "What do you need?"

Dan Younge said: "Three things. In the first place, the Indian word and sign Rylan promised me. In the second place, your consent to go past the sentries."

"That's two," Beer said. "How about the third?"

"I need luck," Dan Younge said.

XXV

It is pleasant to lope a horse across flat country—in the day-time. Under nothing but starlight, when you know there are go-pher holes and prairie dog burrows, it is not so pleasant.

Dan Younge loped anyway.

From time to time he glanced off to the left, towards the vague general direction of the malapie. He didn't think starlight could show him anything there. At any angle that the miners came into town, they'd be a couple of miles away.

Dan Younge looked anyway.

Now he was in the old Indian camp. His muscles tightened between his shoulders, his fingers gripped the reins.

Nothing. Nothing but dead fires, grassless circles where the tents had been. A dead dog. A pile of deer guts from which coy-otes scurried as he came up. A couple of broken travois poles.

Dan Younge loped on through the camp.

There. Something had moved. He fought all the impulses of his body, that wanted to reach for the guns he wasn't wearing, wanted to pull the horse up and dismount, take cover. He rode slowly toward the moving figure, his hands wide, his voice yell-ing, "Friend," in what he hoped wasn't a coward's croak.

When he was almost up on the moving figure, it stopped, and a voice said, "Beer, boss? You got whiskey, mister?"

It was Blanket Moe, the Indian bum who had hung out on Sydnor's porch. How he had gotten out of Rock Spring was a mystery, but not a very big one. He was an Indian, what was left of him, and an Indian was a good man to sneak past picket lines.

The poor old beggar was shuffling along, hunched over. It was probably that he hardly knew what he had said to Dan Younge. He had just uttered his usual request to anyone.

But he was a rat who'd left Rock Spring's sinking ship; and

he was an Indian trying to catch up with his people, so maybe he knew which direction to take.

Dan Younge took a sight over Moe's head, and loped on.

Starlight and stunted sage, some rocks, some mesquite tree. And then, over a rise, firelight and the noise of drums, loud enough to be heard over the thudding of his horse's hooves.

Dan Younge stood up in the saddle, pulled the horse down to a walk, and did an extra-specially good job of keeping his hands clear. He started shouting, "Friend," over and over again, shouting and counting three and shouting again.

Abruptly the drum stopped, and the fire went out, all at once. Someone must have sacrificed a blanket or a buffalo robe to douse a campfire that fast.

Indians don't fight at night. Who said Indians don't fight at night? How did he know?

On the twentieth shout of peace, two sage clumps quickly came to life, and hands grabbed his bridle reins, hands grabbed him around the waist, and he was hauled off his horse.

A voice—young, Indian, unfriendly—said, "Walk so!"

Or maybe it didn't. Maybe that was an Indian word—*wauk-soh*—meaning something like *now you die* or *come eat supper.* He didn't know. He couldn't tell. He went with the young Indian. He said, "Friend, I am a friend," but there was no response.

He was thrust into the firelight, surrounded by Shoshone men. There were no women, no children, no old men in this party, and it didn't take a bright mind to read the meaning of that. Something glinted at a brave's belt, and he looked and saw a freshly-taken scalp, looked further and saw that two other young men had taken trophies too.

That was why Beer had declared martial law, of course; people had been slipping out of Rock Spring. And this was where they had ended up—ornaments on a warrior's belt.

He said: "Nate Allen. I want to talk to Nate Allen."

That got an answer, he guessed. At least one of the Indians said something to the others. Then a brave laughed, and stepped forward and slapped Dan Young across the face.

He said: "Friend. I am a friend. I want to see Nate Allen."

That got an answer too, for what it was worth. A Shoshone grunted something to the others that sounded like Nate Allen's name.

Of course. Squawmen were never called by their names in the tribe. Nate Allen would be something like Grizzlehead or Mushroomeater or Man Who Shot the Bear.

But he had had a little encouragement. They understood him. He said again, "I am a friend. I come in friendship. We have found the ones who killed your people. I can show these killers to you."

They weren't laughing now. He had their attention, and he had to hold it. "Do you know the rocks we call the malapie? The big black rocks? That is where these killers have been hiding. But they will be in our town tonight, the town of the big rock and the spring. You know it. It is where the Indian agent was, Major Miles."

They understood him all right; one of the braves growled. It had been a mistake to mention Miles. The whole tribe was in trouble for killing an Indian agent. But he had to keep talking.

"The soldier sent me out here, the horse soldier with the yellow legs. He says that you can have the killers; we want them dead, too. Then the war will be over."

A voice said, "You make much noise." The accent was not bad.

"I talk words. I am no coward to run away when my town is in trouble. I came to speak true words to the Shoshone."

Nobody answered him this time. He said, "If you would send word to your war chief, on your drums, I will take you to where these killers will be."

Suddenly his wrists were seized, dragged behind him, a rawhide thong bit deep into his flesh. His feet were kicked out from under him, and as he fell, another thong went looping and biting his ankles. He was rolled over on his face.

Somewhere not far away men talked in the Shoshone tongue, and then a drum started talking, too. He was still alive, and the Indians were signaling. Maybe he had won!

And maybe they had decided his scalp was so pretty they'd leave it on his head for some older man to harvest.

XXVI

Beer had had Haley bring the men out of the livery stable and line them up in front of the hotel. Haley called them to attention. Rylan looked them over, and then turned and saluted. "Sir, the command is mustered."

Beer said, "The enemy—the Indians—will attack from that part of the prairie that lies nearest the reservation. Corporal Haley will march you down there, and you will post sentries, form into squads, and in all respects obey Sergeant Haley. That is all."

He turned away quickly, but not too quickly to escape hearing one of the men say, "We're leaving the center part of the town, an' the upper canyon wide open."

Rylan bawled, "Attention! Any more talking in the ranks, an' Sergeant Haley's got my orders to spread eagle the man that talks." He cleared his throat. "Take over, Sergeant."

Private Haley—twice promoted since he had been wounded and therefore made useless for fighting purposes—made harsh noises in his throat, and the men turned raggedly and marched down canyon. He said, "Send Strayne and Lesser with them," and Rylan nodded and thumbed the two nearest troopers after the column.

Mustering the men had, of course, brought the women to the porch of the hotel again. One of them said, clearly, "Sending our men to be killed, and him and his sergeant hanging around here!"

Beer walked slowly into the hotel. The cluster chattered at him, their voices unfriendly, and he cleared his throat. "Mrs. Lea?"

One of the women indicated the staircase. He climbed slowly, to find her alone in the upper hall, sitting in a rocker that she must have dragged from one of the rooms. She looked up and said, "Have you heard from Dan, Mr. Younge?"

He shook his head. "Doesn't mean anything, though. It's much too soon. Where's Mrs. Sydnor?"

Ellen Lea said calmly, "Tied to a bed in that room, and gagged."

Lieutenant Beer chuckled, despite himself. "You're quite a girl," he said. "Dan's lucky."

"So am I," Ellen Lea said, "if he gets back."

The hotel room was like all hotel rooms in the West: splintery tongue-and-groove ceiling, dresser with a cracked marble top, tarnished brass bed, and a wardrobe whose door didn't quite stay closed. There was a smell to it of cheap strong soap and spilled water and sun-scorched resin from the lumber that had been nailed up green and allowed to shrink.

Mrs. Sydnor was on the bed, and again the officer was impressed by Ellen Lea's strength. The lady's ankles were tied together, her wrists were tied to the head of the bed and there was a towel over her mouth. Ellen Lea said, from behind him, "I got tired of listening to her whine."

"Better take the gag out."

Ellen Lea shrugged and slipped past him to the bed. She looked down and said, "You're much more attractive with your mouth tied," but she took the gag off.

Phyllis Sydnor moved her mouth as though she wanted to spit. The first thing she said was, "This is fine gratitude for getting my husband to let you work in the store."

Ellen Lea chuckled slightly. "This is a good time to talk about jobs and stores. But since we are, I worked hard and cheap. The lieutenant wants to talk."

Mrs. Sydnor said, "Thank God you're here."

Beer said, "I'll make it quick. Your husband was here, demanding that you return to him. I think you will be safer here, but I'm leaving the choice up to you."

"Oh, thank you. I knew I could count on you."

He said, "I'm doing you no favor. If the town decides to lynch Sydnor, you will probably be hurt in the riot." That'll make sure he goes, he thought. It had occurred to him that with Sydnor's ammunition the miners could take the town, could stay here, and Dan Younge's plan would fail. Dan Younge would be killed.

A woman bound spread-eagled on a bed is not at her seductive best; but Phyllis Sydnor managed to look alluring and knowing. "I'm not worried about that."

Ellen Lea said sharply, "Because a mob would be men?"

"Why, thanks, Ellen. What a nice thing to say."

Beer turned and ran down the stairs, a spur banging against the steps once and sending a sharp pain through his ankle. He'd done the right thing. With the woman along, the miners would waste no time arguing with Sydnor; they'd be anxious to get back to the malapie and start their celebration. Fresh liquor, supplies and a woman—what bunch of outlaws ever delayed the use of things like that?

XXVII

Dan Younge was on the move. After he'd been thrown down and tied nothing had happened for a while but drumming and talking in the outlandish tongue of the Shoshone; a language that sounded as though every other letter was a K.

Then he had been stood on his feet, pushed over again, kicked. Finally one of the braves had hauled him to his feet and said—in not bad English but with a throaty inflection that made it hard for a battered head to understand—"Why you come?"

Dan Younge kept his own voice steady. It wasn't easy to do. It was hard not to sound angry or afraid or almost anything but steadily self-confident. "I come in peace," he said. "To lead you to the killers of your people."

The Indian said, "You lie."

"All right," Dan Younge said. "Then kill me. And the Shoshone will never find the men who killed their people."

"Huh." This was followed by a series of dialogues in Shoshone. Their tone was not too favorable. One of the young men broke away and came over to Dan Younge. A long knife flicked from the Indian's waist and slashed. It cut through Dan's vest and shirt and just stung the skin on his chest. Then the brave turned back to the argument around the fire.

Good? Bad? Dan was still alive; that they hadn't killed him at once might be a sign that they believed him. Or, it might only mean that the Shoshone, usually peaceful, liked to work up a little heat before they murdered a man.

Then he was forgotten. The arguments all stopped, the Indians all turned. One of them quickly kicked sand on the fire, and three others trotted off into the night.

There wasn't any great mystery about it; their superior ears had heard someone coming.

The news wasn't good. If it had been one of the war parties—best of all, if it had been Nate Allen, the squawman—they would have been told in advance by the drums. He didn't know if Indians had passwords, but they probably did. They wouldn't have sneaked out to surround another war party.

So it was someone from town—Beer, a townsman, Sydnor or Romayne?—and anyone from town that Dan Younge could think of meant bad news.

He didn't have a gun with him; if he had the Indians would have taken it away. But he wondered, if he'd had a gun, would he have blown his brains out now?

The fire still smoldered. The Shoshone men had gone away from it a little way so as not to be targets. They had left him pretty near the fire, unable to move because of his bound ankles. Well, his bound hands were one reason why he wouldn't have committed suicide.

Unexpectedly, laughter sounded out on the prairie, and the three young men came back, pushing Blanket Moe before them. This was the visitor that had so alarmed them, that had scared Dan Younge into wondering about self-destruction!

It was bad enough for life to be violent and treacherous, it didn't have to be a low-comedy joker, too.

One of the men who had stayed with Dan Younge chunked some chamisa roots on the fire and it flared up. In the new light, Dan could see that the young men were laughing now. One of them pushed Blanket Moe in front of Dan.

"Tobacco, mister? Gimme nickel?"

Dan Younge couldn't help it, under the circumstances it was too much. He began to laugh. The Indian grins turned to chuckles and then to roars. Shoshone sense of humor, never far under the surface, had broken through. Dan Younge said, "Loosen my hands so I can get a nickel out."

The boy who spoke English said something in Shoshone, and added, "Gimme nickel," in fair imitation of Blanket Moe's mumble, and then they were all trying to say it.

When the laughter died down, the kid—no longer murderous, they weren't young braves or warpath Indians or warriors but just kids, boys—asked Blanket Moe something. The whiskey bum answered in Shoshone. The one who could speak English said, "Says you're a gambler."

Dan Younge said, "Sure. I gambled you people would listen to me."

"No, a money gambler. Y'ever play the stick game?"

"Mister, I'll gamble on anything."

The boy said: "I'm White Buffalo."

Dan Younge said: "I guess I'm Black Suit."

White Buffalo said: "You sure got guts like Indian." He flicked out his knife, cut the thongs on Dan's wrists and ankles. "Aw, we already drum' fer Bowlegs, you call'm Nate Allen. We jus' have fun with you while we wait."

He added something in Shoshone to his friends. The grunts were not at all threatening now. From outside the circle of firelight, a blanket was produced, more wood was thrown on the fire, some of the boys brought little sticks and bones from out of their breech clouts.

White Buffalo sat down at one side of the blanket, motioning to Dan Younge to sit down at the other. Imitating his host? captor? advisory?—Dan pulled the blanket over his knees. White Buffalo began to sing in a deep bass voice, quite different from the war chants Dan Younge had heard over the prairie. He broke off, "Two bits?"

"Sure," Dan Younge said. "But I don't know the game. You tell me, you speak pretty good English."

"I use' work at agency. You gotta guess what other guy holds."

He went back to chanting, moving his hands under the blanket, weaving back and forth. The other Indians had taken up the chant, too; it seemed to be part of the game. Suddenly White Buffalo flashed a clenched fist above the blanket.

"Two blue sticks and a white bone," Dan Younge said. White

Buffalo opened his hand. There were three bones in it.

Dan Younge fished a quarter out of his pocket, and threw it on the blanket. White Buffalo handed him the sticks and bones, and two other boys slid their legs and hands under the blanket.

Dan Younge hid his hands. He did his best to take up the Shoshone chant; it had a value in distracting your opponent's eyes from your hands. He shuffled awhile, clenched one red stick in his fist, and thrust it out.

"One red stick," White Buffalo said. "You got some funny words in a song, but you sure make a lotta noise. Give the stuff to Kills-two-birds, there."

Dan Younge passed the sticks and bones to the Indian on his right, and went on chanting while he threw another quarter to White Buffalo. Apparently each man played only against the one opposite.

No money except Dan Younge's appeared. This seemed to be a credit arrangement.

They were chanting so hard that Nate Allen—Bowlegs— and his party had ridden up before any of them heard.

The squawman was with the same small group of old chiefs he'd interpreted for at the Agency parley. He dropped off his horse, spat in the roaring fire and said: "You sure went Injun in a hurry, gambler. Never can get the people to put out night guards, but you oughta know better."

Dan Younge started to get up, and the pile of quarters in front of White Buffalo jingled. Nate Allen grinned his tight, tired grin and said: "Betcha you didn't win onct. I was playing th' peyon game five years afore I won."

"I ought to take you up on that bet," Dan Younge said. "I won two out of seven throws."

"Yeah?" Nate Allen chuckled and said something to the two old chiefs who still sat their horses. They laughed, and one of them said something to White Buffalo that made all the Shoshone laugh.

Dan Younge was counting heads. There were almost forty

Indians here now. Three or four times more than there were miners, he figured, even with Sydnor and Romayne and maybe one or two more townsmen thrown in. But the chiefs and some of the other riders were pretty old to be fighting.

He said, "Nate, I didn't come here to gamble. The lieutenant sent me out. He declared military law in Rock Spring. We had a fight, some of us, with the men who killed your Shoshone, murdered some wagon people, white people, too. He's given me authority to tell your people that they can have these men, they're outlaw miners, and he'll call it square."

"White men turning white men over to the Indians?"

"The lieutenant's got his back against a wall and he knows it."

"It's not up to me," Nate Allen said. He turned and the firelight was strong on the curved legs that had given him his Indian name. He talked to the two chiefs.

Dan Younge watched White Buffalo's face. He felt, somehow, that he and the young Indians were friends, now. I learned from him, he thought. Do me a lot of good. That peyon game would go over big in San Francisco.

The chiefs were talking now, first one and then another. Dan Younge felt in his pocket, brought out his sack of makings, creased a paper carefully. From out of nowhere, Blanket Moe was at his side. "Tobacco, mister?"

"Gimme a neekel," Dan Younge said. White Buffalo's eyes were on him. He finished building his own cigarette and passed the sack across, and White Buffalo took it, fished a smoking stick—just a straight hollow tube of willow—out of his waistband and filled it with Dan Younge's tobacco.

As they bent to get coals to light up, White Buffalo said softly—the chiefs were still pow-wowing—"We gamble good together, Black Suit. Maybe we fight good together, too."

And that was how Dan Younge knew that the Shoshone had agreed to the deal.

XXVIII

Now a watery, pale crescent of moon rose in the prairie sky. A light wind came with it, crosswise to the path of their journey, and in the pale moonlight Dan Younge could see as he rode with bent head the breeze whipping the dust away from their horses' hooves.

He swung his reins, and his horse rode closer to old Nate Allen. Despite the violent rush of their passage, the old squaw-man rose like a staff from his ancient flick-forked saddle. His neck and back were both stiff, exposing his unblinking eyes to whatever sand and grit and wind the night might bring them.

Dan Younge said, "There's this passage way under the rock. They'll come out of there, if they haven't already, and they'll come out in single file. If we start shooting too soon, they'll go back in, which is too bad."

"Go back in and be murdered by the people there, shot by the Army?"

"Rock Spring's a nest of scared men, the Army's down to a handful. We know these miners are going to tie up with a couple of townsmen who'll tell them that. No, once they know the Indians are out here, they won't be afraid to go back in. So—if your Indians could just use their bows and arrows on the first few, keep it quiet, we'd stand a better chance."

Nate Allen didn't answer.

Dan Younge looked up, looked around. "We're drifting a little to the West."

He was sure that the old man heard him, because Nate Allen's horse moved in the right direction. They were leading the column, Nate and Dan and White Buffalo. The old chiefs had stayed behind, leaving the war party to the braves.

Suddenly Nate Allen spoke. "These are Shoshone. They're

not Pawnee or Apache or Comanche. Ah, they fight, but they don't like it, like some other people do. Naw, we gotta let them work 'emselves up, with whooping, an' shootin' off guns an' riding fast in a circle. Does something to an Indian, all that foofaraw, changes him into somethin' different."

"I don't even have a knife with me," Dan Younge said. "Not to mention any kind of gun."

Nate Allen spat again. Then he sighed, and shifted for the first time in the ride in his saddle. "Injuns is funny," he said. "Sometimes I think mebbe so I woulda made a better life with the whites. Don't know. Never tried it. I'll git you a knife, an' you better do like'n I say. Happen you don't, these people are likely to git so worked up they forget your good advice an' guiding, an' they'll finish the battle with no white man lef' in the saddle. They don't think of me as white, often."

He raised his voice and called something in Shoshone. The words were repeated back down the loping column of ponies.

White Buffalo rode into Dan Younge from the other side, and reached out to hand Dan Younge a hunting knife. "Chief!" he said. "Big Chief!"

Now the country was breaking up a little, becoming choppy instead of rolling. They couldn't be far from the back of the big rock. There was even a slight smell of water in the air from the municipal spring.

Dan Younge said, "We'd better wait here."

Again Nate Allen passed the word back and the party halted. There were none of the noises made when a party of white men stopped on the prairie. If any of the Indians owned metal bits, they had discarded them for the warpath. No bridle jingled, there were no shod horses to stamp. Dan Younge leaned forward and rested his hand on his horse's nose, as he saw the Indians doing, to stop any whickering.

It was nervy, waiting. He said to Nate Allen, "I thought Indians didn't fight at night."

"Some tribes don't. This one does. Hush up, now."

It was the pony that warned him first that company was coming. The smooth nostrils under his hand wrinkled as the animal was urged to greet his kind.

"Now," he said. "Now."

White Buffalo said: "Ya!" His voice was as soft wind over young grass.

They came, then, the renegades, and they were noisy and bold in their coming. Perhaps they too believed that Indians didn't fight at night, which proved the danger in regarding an Indian as an Indian and not recognizing his differences...

Dan Younge's party was down in a little swale. The miners passed them on a ridge. More than one of the passing silhouettes had a bent arm and a bottle to catch the weak moonlight.

If Charley Sydnor was among them, Dan Younge couldn't tell. Some of the miners were fat men, too. And if Jack Romayne was there, he couldn't be sure, for there were straight-backed young miners, too.

But then a passing rider lifted an arm, and Dan Younge gasped. The sleeve of no miner's riding habit ended in a frothy lace cuff, the bosom of no renegade swelled so interestingly.

It was obvious that Sydnor had brought or sent a woman out with the miners, as a bribe or because he really thought a woman would be safer in a renegade camp than in besieged Rock Spring.

But what woman? Dan Younge had no way of knowing anything that had happened in town after he rode out. Ellen could have listened to Jack Romayne; he didn't think so, but few people want to die, and the spirit of Rock Spring had been one of certain death.

The riders were still passing on the skyline, but there was a petering out. Soon it would be time to strike, and the Shoshone expected him to render the first blow. If he didn't, the Indians would consider that he'd been trying to lead them into a trap, and they'd drift away. Undoubtedly they'd kill him first.

It probably wasn't Ellen Lea up there, but it was a woman.

Phyllis Sydnor had been his lady for several months; it was impossible to erase past tenderness from his memory.

Impossible to erase other things, too. Stories heard over the table of what Indians did to white women. They were harder on them than on white men, because women gave birth to more whites, to drive the Indians from their land...

Nate Allen turned to him. "That's all of 'em, gambler."

White Buffalo's hand came out of the dark. "Strike hard, Black Suit."

It was now. It was himself or a woman up there, a woman—either one—who did mean or had meant a good deal to him. It was the way a man felt about women, when all the cynicism of a gambler's life was stripped away.

It was—hell—the people of Rock Spring, and it was time to ride.

He pulled his fingers back from his horse's nose, swung his legs hard back into the animal's flank, and was up the ridge in one long bound almost before he could get his knife from his rein hand to his right one.

The man to strike was the last one in line. Leave the Indians to head off the column, keep it from escaping into the malapie.

He was in among the stragglers on the horse's third bound, his spurs still raking back, his legs swinging. He had a glimpse of a white moustached face, surprising under a dark hat brim. He smelt the reek of cheap whiskey, and then his knife hand swung down, and the miner screamed.

Listen to that, Shoshone! Hear that, Bowlegs and White Buffalo and all the rest of you Indians. Hear that, and figure out whose side I'm on.

His knife was still in the miner. It was a good knife White Buffalo had given him, it pulled out easy. The renegade was falling from the saddle, and Indian ponies were drumming up the ridge and he rode hard and slashed at the next miner and missed and nearly went out of the saddle.

It saved his life. A pistol went off close enough for the powder to burn his rein hand.

The Shoshone should have been among the miners by now, killing, helping him kill. But they weren't, and he was in bad trouble, and he knew why.

The Indians were circling the column, tying it down, riding around and around the stalled-up renegades. The braves had gone down on the far side of their ponies, hanging on by one leg and a grip on the mane.

Well, that was fine, but he had their enemy stopped for them and...

He remembered what Nate Allen had said. They needed to work themselves up. Killing didn't come easy to Shoshone people.

He had not been still while he thought, he'd been kneeing his horse away from the milling renegades. Maybe in the dark and at a little distance, he'd pass for a miner himself.

The Indians were whooping now. Come on, you braves, come on, White Buffalo, Nate Allen! Cut in here!

He was, he found, comparatively safe from the miners. Their attention was all on the encircling warriors. The renegades were pulling their horses in, facing out, and he got himself into the pattern.

Occasionally a miner would fire out at the galloping ring around them. He couldn't see that any damage was being done. No pony faltered in his stride, and even an Indian pony would stop that circling if his rider was knocked off.

He couldn't understand why the Indians were holding their fire. They had herded the miners into a tight and easy target. Then suddenly an Indian cut away from the war band and dashed into the knot of whites. His arm was a flash of silver in the moonlight, up and down, and then up again.

He was trying to get a renegade with his blade!

Dan Younge had heard, someplace, sometime, that some Indians—it was as vague as that—got merit or coup or whatever they called it only for enemies killed by hand, not by arrow or rifle. He hadn't known it was these, the Shoshone. If he ever got out of this, he was going to make an awful close study of Indians, and how to tell one tribe from another, and what to expect.

Men were shooting, many men, at the charging Indian. It seemed incredible that they didn't kill him, but the truth was, a head-on horse and man is not much target, and the outlaws had bunched up too close in their fear. Each man's horse jostled the others, and their bullets went wide.

Then there was a scream from behind him, on the other side of the bunch, and Dan Younge turned his head. A horse was rearing high there, and the moonlight caught his neck for a moment and sparkled brightly on what must be blood.

Another one-man charge, and it seemed to have worked. The horse, still screaming, went down, and there was a human shout and then a Shoshone yell that sounded triumphant.

The bunch broke then, each man for himself, each horse, in truth, carrying a commandless rider out of there, away from that spot where horses screamed and died and the smells were the bad ones of human blood and gunpowder.

Dan Younge let Ranger take him out. He wasn't sure he could have stopped the horse. He was glad to get away from the renegades before they saw who he was.

But then he saw the Shoshone fanning out of their circle, and he realized that they had been using tactics. They had risked two men to break up the bunched renegades and, now outnumbering the whites, had every chance of running them down and slaughtering them, knife to back.

There were two Indians riding after each of the men who had burst out of the grouped stand. Two Indians riding, each with a knife, some with the knife held in their rein hands, and their long spears held aloft in the other hand.

Dan Younge pulled up. Though he was unmistakably overdressed for an Indian, perhaps by not fleeing he could get himself identified as the friend and guide of the Shoshone, instead of as enemy.

The little moon went behind a cloud, then, and he groaned. He whipped off his hat, surest sign of a white man, and made his horse hold still. But it wasn't easy; men aren't built neither to run from danger or fight it.

Ranger fidgeted as horses flew by him.

Then the moon came out again, and a voice came from a galloping figure: "That's that damned gambler," and a bullet was fired from the figure's gun. It sounded like Sydnor; it had Sydnor's bulk. The gallop caused it to miss.

Whoever it was, the fat man went another fifty feet and then two Shoshone were on him, their light weight and saddleless ponies giving them speed. A knife and a spear rose and fell, and the big figure went out of the saddle.

An Indian pulled up and dropped down, and the other went in, his bloody spear shining, to look for more blood.

The dismounted Indian was using his knife, and now he stood, braced a foot against the downed white man and tugged. The Shoshone were scalping.

He must have expected that, but he was shocked anyway. Those men on the ground were of his own race, and he had caused this to happen to them.

Another horse loped by him, pulled up, came back. A voice said: "Dan," without emphasis.

It was Phyllis Sydnor. She was riding side-saddle—though most Rock Spring women contented themselves with a boy's saddle and a split skirt—and in the bad light, she looked immaculate, dressed for a St. Louis Boulevard. She said, "What are you doing here?"

He heard his voice grow heavily sardonic; his old tone with his ladies. "Admiring my handiwork. I'm in the position of guide, counselor, and dearest friend to our copper skinned brethren."

"My God, Dan."

"And you, dear lady?"

"Lieutenant Beer let me go back to my husband. He...we

thought we'd be better making a run for it. I guess we were wrong."

Dan Younge said, "Unless I'm much mistaken, yonder lies your husband. I'd not bother to look at him. He's balder than usual."

She said: "Dan—if you're the Indians' friend—"

She didn't finish the sentence, but instead rode nearer, dropped a hand on his bridle hand. He said, "Take your glove off, you'll be more effective that way. I'm afraid we've altered your plans. If my allies and I hadn't shown up, by now you'd be queen of the carnival in the malapie. You knew that, didn't you? Those miners were not planning to put you on an alabaster pedestal."

The breeze was blowing, and bringing with it the most horrible kinds of sounds. Sounds of Shoshone war whoops, sounds of slaughtered horses screaming, sounds of men dying, and not stoically. But Phyllis Sydnor sat her horse, and seemed to show no interest in the world around her. She managed, from her clumsy side seat, to keep the restive animal quiet, and was quiet herself. She said, "I have never had any trouble getting what I needed from men, and I expected no trouble from the outlaws that I would not have welcomed as preferable to certain death in Rock Spring."

"That's as true as you've ever talked."

"It's as near death as I've ever been."

He shifted his weight, and his horse sidestepped and took him away from her hand. Hooves drummed towards them, and she said, "You're sure the Indians are your friends?"

He said, "No," or thought he did. He was busy wheeling his horse. Two dark figures bored down on them at a gallop, and he clenched White Buffalo's knife.

But it was White Buffalo and Nate Allen, Bowlegs. The latter said, "So you're still alive, gambler?"

Dan Younge said: "I stood still. Your boys seemed to prefer a moving target."

Nate Allen said, "You're a cool one."

"You took coup on a fat man," White Buffalo said. "Here."

He fumbled at his belt, and held out something. Dan Younge took a quick look and said, "White Buffalo is a good friend. I give him my coup to remember me by."

White Buffalo said, "Got four already."

"Take one more and be my brother," Dan Younge said. So it had been a fat man he had killed, at the beginning of the battle. Well, it hadn't been Sydnor.

The fighting was widely scattered now, far from them, in little scattered knots. Any screams that could be heard at this distance were probably those of horses.

"What now?" Nate Allen asked. He and White Buffalo had been eyeing the lady out of their slanted eyes; but neither had mentioned her.

"Clean up," Dan Younge said. "Wipe those renegades off the prairie... Did you see a man with a star, a sheriff, with them?"

This was too much for White Buffalo; he asked something in Shoshone. Nate Allen answered, and then turned to Dan Younge. "Kills-no-deer got him. He's got the badge twisted in his horse's mane."

Dan Younge said, "Good. Tomorrow, come into town. Not more than five men, maybe you two and a young chief and two old chiefs... We'll make a peace treaty."

He held out the knife White Buffalo had given him. "Here, and thanks."

"Keep it, brother." White Buffalo watched while Dan picked up his reins, turned his horse's head towards town. "What of the woman, Black Suit?"

"Keep her, brother."

Phyllis Sydnor let out a yelp. White Buffalo said, "I do not use white women."

Dan Younge said, "All right, lady. Back into town with me. Unless you want her, Nate."

"Too old," Nate Allen said. "I got me a squaw and I'm living peaceful. I aim to keep it that way."

Dan Younge said, "Come on, then. I suppose you own Sydnor's store now."

"There's not much in it," Phyllis said. "He sold a lot of stock to the miners... I suppose the Indians have it now."

"Sue them," Dan Younge said.

"He got gold for it," Phyllis Sydnor said.

Dan Younge snorted. "Come on. That wasn't very bright of him. If he hadn't had their gold on him, he might have had a chance in the malapie—if we'd let you get there."

The lady said, "It's on him, in a money belt."

Dan Younge swore. "All right, lady," he said. "We're three men here, and you can do anything with men; you told me so. So what you can do with us is we will let you go search your dead husband, but we won't help you. He fell right over there."

She stared at him a moment, and then she rode away, elegant on her side saddle, her long skirt sweeping down the side of her horse.

"If she gets down," Dan Younge said, "I'll be damned if I see how she's going to get up again in that rig."

Nate Allen said, "You're a tough one, gambler."

"She helped in making me that way."

White Buffalo said: "We don't make so much of our women."

They watched her, walking her horse towards Sydnor's corpse. The distant cries were dying out now; perhaps all the miners were dead. More likely the Shoshone were getting glutted with their kill, were suffering the reaction of normally peaceful people after a fight.

An occasional pony was coming back to them, its rider jumping down now and then to loot a corpse.

Phyllis Sydnor stopped by her husband, and was agile sliding down the side of her horse. She knelt there.

Two Indians, bearing lances, drifted their ponies up out of a roll in the prairie. At first it looked as though their aimless course would make them miss the Sydnors, living and dead, but first one and then the other of the lancers turned that way.

Dan Younge picked up his reins and swung his spurred boots. But Nate Allen on one side and White Buffalo on the other caught his reins. "They kill you, too," White Buffalo said, "Now, when they are on warpath."

And Nate Allen said, "You're not so tough, gambler," and held on hard to Dan's horse while Dan struggled to break loose. Somehow White Buffalo had taken back the knife of brotherhood he had given Dan Younge; there was nothing the gambler could do.

There was no noise on the prairie. The lances lifted and sunk and the Indians rode on, almost negligently, sated with killing. They didn't even bother to take what would have been a notable scalp.

"We'll take you to the edge of town," Nate Allen said. "An' see you don't do nothing foolish."

So Dan Younge went back to Rock Spring. And Ellen Lea. And respectability.

www.ingramcontent.com/pod-product-compliance
Lightning Source LLC
Chambersburg PA
CBHW020145180626
46810CB00004B/1731